FLOODS

7

Top Gear

THE FLOODS

7

Top Gear

Colin Thompson

illustrations by the author

RANDOM HOUSE AUSTRALIA

This work is fictitious. Any resemblance to anyone living or dead is purely coincidental. You should be so lucky.

A Random House book
Published by Random House Australia Pty Ltd
Level 3, 100 Pacific Highway, North Sydney NSW 2060
www.randomhouse.com.au

First published by Random House Australia in 2008

Addresses for companies within the Random House Group can be found at www.randomhouse.com.au/offices.

National Library of Australia
Cataloguing-in-Publication Entry

Thompson, Colin (Colin Edward).
Top gear.

For primary school age.
ISBN 978 1 74166 254 2 (pbk.).

1. Title. (Series: Thompson, Colin (Colin Edward). Floods; 7).

A823.3

Design, illustration and typesetting by Colin Thompson
Additional typesetting by Anna Warren, Warren Ventures
Printed and bound by Griffin Press

Random House Australia uses papers that are natural, renewable and recyclable products and made from wood grown in sustainable forests. The logging and manufacturing processes are expected to conform to the environmental regulations of the country of origin.

14

Winchflat has now decided to be 39 because that's how old his brain is. Satanella is now 287 because she says her brain is much cleverer than Winchflat's. Which of course it isn't.

For my grandson Walter

who, at the age of two, knows the meaning of the word ONOMATOPOEIA.

Well, actually he doesn't. He knows the word, but he hasn't the faintest idea what it means, which is probably why he's never actually used it in a sentence.

Whereas his baby brother

Donald,

at six months old, knows exactly what an ONOMATOPOEIA is. It is something you put in your mouth and eat, but then so is everything.

Like, the story so far, man . . .

Lots and lots of brilliant, fascinating, exciting, slightly naughty, environmentally friendly, hybrid, chocolate-covered, very fast, hydroponic, biodegrading stuff has happened, ending up with the VERY EVIL Hearse Whisperer – the favourite spy of Mordonna Flood's father, the King of Transylvania Waters – almost, but not quite, catching the ENTIRE Flood family.

While they were away on holiday at the smart seaside town of Port Folio with their human friends the Hulberts, the Hearse Whisperer totally

destroyed their home back in Acacia Avenue. So now the Floods are on the run again . . .

AND there is now a new addition to the Floods family. No, Mordonna has not had another baby. Valla married the stunningly beautiful Mildred Flambard, who was burnt at the stake as a witch in 1803.

This all means that the following story will be brilliant, fascinating, and full of extremely naughty and not at all environmentally friendly swear words that you will never have heard before.

When the Floods had decided to go on the run, none of them could agree where to go so the Hearse Whisperer wouldn't find them. They had rented a minibus and driven away from Port Folio without the slightest idea where they were going.

To cover their tracks they decided to dump the minibus and get another vehicle.

'That's what they do in the movies,' said Betty. 'Then they set fire to the old vehicle to get rid of their fingerprints and any forensic evidence.'

'Can I do the fire?' said Merlinmary.

'We're witches and wizards, remember,' said Mordonna. 'We don't have fingerprints.'

'Yeah, but Mum,' said Merlinmary, who loved burning things, 'what about the forensic stuff like hairs and bits of dead skin?'

'We can cast a spell that will make all the evidence look like the bus had been driven by a Belgian girls' hockey team,' said Mordonna.

'Oh, Mum.'

'We are not having a fire,' Mordonna insisted.

So they drove into a dark forest where Mordonna turned the minibus into a pumpkin. Obviously their arch-enemy, the Hearse Whisperer, had not fitted a tracking device to it, or she would now be trying to turn them into small blocks of charcoal. But it was agreed you could never be too careful.

'A pumpkin's a bit risky, isn't it?' said Betty. 'I mean, supposing Cinderella comes along and her fairy godmother tries to turn it into a silver coach? Won't it turn back into a minibus?'

'I think that's a risk we could live with,' said Mordonna with a smile, but to make Betty feel happier she turned the pumpkin into a Belgian telephone directory.

'But supposing someone from Belgium is on holiday here and hiking through the woods, which I believe Belgian people love to do, and they want to phone home but can't remember the number?' Betty protested.

'OK, OK, I'll make it a Tristan da Cunha telephone directory.'

'But . . .'

'All right, a packet of liquorice dog biscuits and Satanella can –'

'Hey, come on,' said Satanella. 'Do I look stupid? Only stupid creatures eat liquorice.'

'Oh, for goodness sake,' said Mordonna. 'You children are so picky. Who would have thought it would be so difficult to get rid of a minibus?'

In the end she turned it into something smelly, brown and disgusting, which most people who

have any taste would flush down the lavatory.[1]

'There, no one will go near that,' she said.

'But in Australia they spread that on bread,' Betty began. Mordonna gave her a don't-you-dare-say-another-word look before she could say another word.

Then they sent Valla and Mildred out to get a new van. This was not a good idea because they came back with a hearse.

'Sweetheart,' said Mordonna, 'it's a gorgeous hearse, exactly the sort of vehicle that our family should have, but there's a couple of reasons why you have to take it back.'

'Oh?' said Valla, who had gone through a lot of trouble to get the hearse.

'Firstly, it's exactly the sort of vehicle the Hearse Whisperer would expect us to be driving.

---

[1] *In Australia they put it in jars and sell it to other people to spread on their toast. I'm not allowed to say what it is in case we get sued, but it rhymes with 'Make sure the lid is done up incredibly tight.' This, of course, should say, 'Make sure the lid is done up incredibly tightly', but that wouldn't rhyme with Vegemite.*

In fact, I wouldn't be at all surprised if she hadn't bugged every single hearse in the country, including this one, so you'd better get rid of it as quickly as you can.'

'And the other reason?' said Valla, who was now sulking.

'I am not spending day after day with all my kids bickering over whose turn it is to lie on the coffin table.'

'OK, I'll take it back.'

'There's a third thing,' said Mordonna as Valla climbed into the driving seat.

'What?'

'Who's in the coffin in the back?'

'Oops.'

Finally, Nerlin went off and came back with a VW campervan with lots of flowers painted all over it.

'I thought we could disguise ourselves as hippies,' he said. 'After all, some of us kind of look a bit hippyish already.'

'Speak for yourself, Daddy,' said Betty. 'I don't.'

This was perfectly true. Betty looked like something out of *The Sound of Music* – sweet and blonde and pretty – but the rest of the family did look like hippies, or rather hippies crossed with goths crossed with emos. Except Valla and Mildred, who just looked like hippies who had been dead for a long time and then turned into zombies.

'What, you mean we have to stop washing and combing our hair?' said one of the twins.

'Yes,' said Nerlin.

'Cool,' said Merlinmary. 'I'll have dreadlocks by tomorrow.'

'I wouldn't do that if I were you,' said Winchflat. 'I mean, if your hair gets really matted up you might end up getting a short circuit and giving yourself a nasty electric shock.'

'I suppose we should dress like hippies too,' said Mordonna. 'All sort of . . . floaty and cheesecloth.'

'Cheesecloth? I want one that's had that really stinky blue cheese wrapped in it,' said Morbid.

'I don't think it's actually had cheese wrapped up in it,' said Mordonna. 'I think it just looks like the same stuff they use.'

'Well, could we have some cheese on ours?' said Morbid.

'If you're having cheese, I'd like some beef fat rubbed into my fur,' said Satanella.

By the time they'd all finished dressing up they smelled like a delicatessen.

Then of course there were the beads and the chains and the bells, which were mostly OK except

Valla was wearing a genuine antique bell that had been used to summon dead bodies during the Great Plague. He insisted on ringing it every time they passed a graveyard, which then meant some of the older skeletons got very distressed and poked their arms up through the grass.

'What else do we have to do?' asked Betty.

'Well, apparently we have to call each other "man" and say "like" a lot,' said Nerlin.

'Man? But I'm a woman,' said Mordonna.

'Yes, I know,' said Nerlin. 'Hippies are weird. Or should I say, like, hippies are, like, weird, man.'

'Far out, man,' said Winchflat. He had a friend at Quicklime College, Rivermoon Cuspidor, who was one of the very few hippy wizards, so he already knew some of the lingo.

'What is?' said Nerlin.

'What is what?'

'What is far out?'

'I don't know,' said Winchflat. 'It's just something you say . . . man.'

As the sun set, they said their final goodbyes to the Hulberts and drove away from Port Folio into an uncertain future. They knew where they couldn't be safe: everywhere. And they knew where they could be safe: nowhere.

Although Nerlin had been the one who had driven the first minibus, none of the Floods could actually drive. It had been decided that Nerlin would be the safest because his brain worked slower than anyone else's – almost as slow as some very clever humans – so he would be less likely to go too fast. Winchflat had made a Do-Everything-Except-The-Steering-Wheel-Machine, which he had taken out of the minibus and fitted into the VW so all Nerlin had to do was look in the direction they wanted to go. This caused a few problems at first until Nerlin learnt to stop himself looking at all the sheep and trees as they passed them.

Everyone drew straws to see who would sit in the front passenger seat. The one with the shortest straw sat next to Nerlin and kept poking him in the arm to make him concentrate, while everyone else

sat in the back of the van either facing backwards or with their eyes shut.

'Where are we going?' asked Betty.

Nerlin pulled over onto the side of the road and scratched his head.

'Good point,' he said. 'I hadn't actually thought about that. Anyone have any ideas?'

'Well, where is the most obvious place the Hearse Whisperer will be expecting us to go?' said Mordonna.

'Far, far away,' said Nerlin.

'Exactly,' Mordonna answered. 'So we should go as far away from far, far away as possible.'

'Which is where?'

'Here.'

'Right,' said Nerlin, not convinced. 'But we've only driven five hundred metres.'

'Well, it'll save on petrol,' said Betty.

'But isn't that exactly what the Hearse Whisperer will be expecting us to do?' said Valla. 'I mean, she's incredibly clever. She's bound to work out that here is as far away from where we probably think she probably thinks we would go.'

'Half-past three,' said Merlinmary, who had completely lost track of the conversation.

'True,' said Mordonna. 'In that case we should go somewhere that is almost – but not exactly, in case she works that out too – halfway between here and far, far away.'

'That's probably the best idea,' said Winchflat. 'And we do have one advantage.'

'What's that then?'

'The Hearse Whisperer doesn't know where here is.'

'Well, actually,' said Valla, 'she knows where *her* here is, but not where ours is.'

'So that would mean that her far, far away is a different place from our far, far away,' Mildred Flambard-Flood added. 'So in actual fact we would be quite safe going to far, far away.'

'You're absolutely right,' said Mordonna. 'Clever girl. I knew you were the perfect choice for Valla to marry.'

This was the first time Mildred had made a contribution to family discussions and both she and Valla glowed with pride at Mordonna's praise, in a way that only semi-dead corpses with paper-thin skin can glow, which is very bright red as though they had swallowed a traffic light.

'But no safer than staying here,' said Betty.

'Or going to halfway between here and the far, far away place,' said Satanella.

'There is one place this Hearse Whisperer creature would never imagine we would go,'

Mildred added. 'Transylvania Waters. And anyway, from what you all say, it sounds like paradise and I would love to go there.'

'But we'd have to be mad to go there . . .' Nerlin began.

'That's why she'd never imagine we would.'

'You are absolutely right, Mildred,' beamed Mordonna. 'And you know, if the truth be told, I've been getting the odd homesick twinge recently.'

'So have I,' said Valla, 'and I've never even been there.'

'Us too,' said the twins.

It turned out they all missed Transylvania Waters, even the old bird Parsnip.

'Snip-Snip black twigs miss,' he said, which really summed up everyone's feelings.

Anyone born in Transylvania Waters will understand this yearning for home. It is a country so unlike any other, a country so damp and weird that its power is stored in every cell of every Transylvanian's body. No matter how many

generations have passed since their ancestors left the country, this power never dies.[2]

Everyone felt homesick except the Queen. All through this discussion, Queen Scratchrot had sat folded up in her Dead-Granny-Backpack under one of the seats. There had been no time to collect her goat's wool blanket from the hotel laundry and to cushion her fragile bones against the bumps in the road, so Winchflat had emptied six cartons of pot noodles into the backpack. The van was filled with the smell of Instant Chicken Chow Mein mixed with fifteen food additives and the unmistakeable scent of a body that had been buried and dug up again quite a lot of times.

The poor Queen was torn up with mixed emotions. Part of her[3] yearned to return to the land of her birth, as long as she didn't have to be

---

[2] *If you are somewhere lush and green and it begins to rain and that incredible rich damp smell comes out of the earth and fills the air and you feel something stir deep in your soul, then somewhere in your family tree, maybe hundreds of years ago, you have a relative who came from Transylvania Waters.*

[3] *Her left knee, right ankle and both thumbs.*

anywhere near the King, but another part of her[4] was devastated at the thought of leaving the country where her true love was imprisoned.

'I am not homesick,' she said. 'In fact, were I to go home now, it would make me very sick indeed.'

'Why is that, Mother?' Mordonna asked.

'Well, I need hardly say that the last person I ever want to see again is your father,' said the Queen. 'But my heart aches at the thought of leaving the

4 *Both elbows, several ribs and nose.*

country where my one true love is held trapped in a cage like some defenceless wild animal.'[5]

'Yes, of course, Mother,' said Mordonna. 'We cannot even think of leaving here without first rescuing Vessel.'

The others all nodded. This was something they tried not to think about. They knew they would have to save Vessel, but they also knew how incredibly dangerous it would probably be.

'Don't worry, Granny,' Betty whispered into her grandmother's backpack. 'We'll think of something.'

'Of course,' said Mordonna, 'that is the place above all others where the Hearse Whisperer is most likely to be waiting for us.'

'Could we not somehow convince her that we had fled and deserted him?' said Valla.

'Maybe, but I doubt we could fool her.'

---

[5] *The Queen was, of course, referring to Vessel, her old servant and secret love, who the Hearse Whisperer had trapped inside an enchanted birdcage. You can read about this in* The Floods 3: Home & Away.

'Don't worry, Granny,' said Winchflat, still feeling the pain from losing his beloved Igorina.[6] 'We will find a way to rescue your sweetheart.'

'There's a good boy,' said the Queen, tapping Winchflat on the ankle.

'First we need somewhere safe to hide,' said Nerlin, 'so we can work out a rescue plan.'

'Let's try and find a hippy encampment,' said Mordonna. 'Somewhere we can try and blend in.'

Blending in anywhere for the Floods was about as likely as a stick of dynamite blending in with a bonfire.

They drove inland until they reached soft green rolling hills and little valleys of quaint villages full of rich city slickers who were 'reassessing and changing their lives in a deep and meaningful way by leaving the hustle and bustle of the city for a tranquil life in the country', which meant what they were actually doing was

---

6 *See* The Floods 4: Survivor *to learn how Winchflat built himself a girlfriend and* The Floods 6: The Great Outdoors *to read how he lost her.*

taking all the city stuff with them, but with more flowers.

'This is pretty,' said Mordonna.

'I know – horrible, isn't it?' said Betty.

'Don't think we'll find many hippies around here,' said Winchflat. 'In fact, I think if we stopped they'd chase us out of town.'

'So how do we actually find some hippies?' said Valla.

'Well, I thought if we could find one of these commune things where they all live together in a muddy field full of old buses and vans, we could hide out there for a while until we work out exactly what to do,' said Winchflat.

'Yes, but how do we find a commune?'

'Maybe it would be easier to avoid all the places where we would never find one,' said Valla. 'Like here in golf club paradise. I mean, even the grass is standing neatly to attention here.'

'Good idea, sweetheart,' said Mordonna. She turned to her husband, who had managed to drive for over three kilometres without hitting anything

or leaving the road. 'Are we not blessed to have such wonderfully clever and talented children, my darling?'

'Indeed we are,' said Nerlin, who knew which side of the family their kids had got their brains from. 'Do you think it's catching? Because I could do with a bit more clever.'

They drove down more winding country lanes that gradually stopped winding, and through more soft green valleys that gradually stopped being soft and green, and began climbing until they came out onto a wide flat moorland where the trees were no more than scrubby bushes and the earth huddled in small piles between big grey rocks. There were no houses here, no fences, no telephone wires, almost no sign that humans had ever set foot there, apart from a few scruffy sheep that were attempting to eat the last scrappy bits of green in this desolate place.

'This is more like it,' said Valla. 'No one would live up here if they could afford not to.'

'Though, of course, humans must have been

here at some point,' said Betty. 'Otherwise there wouldn't even be a road.'

'Yes,' said Mordonna. 'And a road has a beginning and an end so it must go somewhere.'

'If you ask me,' said Valla, looking out at the endless expanse of desolation, 'it looks like the road to nowhere.'

Which was a Very Wise thing to say, because they drove between some huge boulders, turned a corner and there, pointing down a dirt track off into the distance, was a sign.

It said:

NOWHERE

'Now, that's my kind of place,' said Valla and they turned off down the track.

The track to Nowhere led up into a range of bleak mountains. Its surface was covered in rock and potholes and deep puddles, yet there were tyre tracks in the mud that looked to be fairly recent. The small clumps of scrubby grass that had clung to the side of the road gradually vanished until everything, as far

as the eye could see, was grey and lifeless.

'This is my kind of countryside,' said Valla. 'No nasty flowers and pretty stuff, just a grey lifeless expanse.'

'Just like you, my darling,' said Mildred.

'You too, cuddlecorpse,' said Valla.

'Yeuuch,' said Betty.

Then the signs began.

At first they were faint, like chalk that had been rained on. The first one, on a rock half-sunk into the ground, said:

THE ROAD TO NOWHERE

It was followed almost immediately by another that said:

'Do you think we should go back?' said Betty.

'No. They look ancient,' said Winchflat. 'Probably been there for years.'

The next sign did not look ancient. It was on a white metal post and in neat black paint it said:

'I had a great-aunt called Anthrax,' said Mordonna.

'They've spelt dangerous wrong,' said Betty.

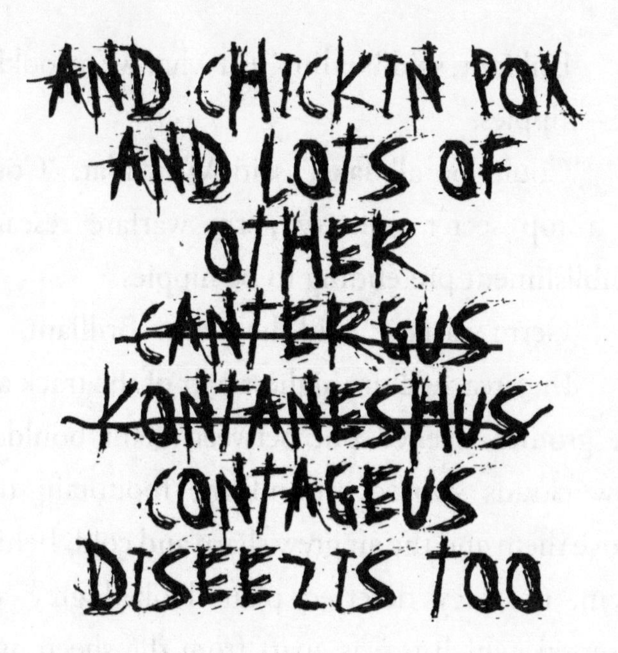

said the next sign.

said the next, followed by:

‘Brilliant, said Nerlin. ‘Just what we’re looking for – hippies.’

‘Could be all fake,’ said Winchflat. ‘Could be a top secret military germ warfare research establishment pretending to be hippies.’

‘Germ warfare?’ said the twins. ‘Brilliant.’

They reached the highest part of the track and the ground levelled out between giant boulders. Low clouds swirled around the mountain tops above them and the air grew sharp and cold. Behind them, the grey deserted plain looked grey and deserted, which it was apart from the sheep, who didn’t count because sheep are more like walking vegetables than proper thinking creatures.

There was one last sign.

‘I would say,’ said Nerlin, pulling over, ‘that whoever lives up here does not want visitors.’

‘You think?’ said Betty.

‘Well, nothing we’ve seen so far is any risk to us,’ said Mordonna. ‘Don’t forget we’re witches and wizards. Bombs and diseases have no effect on us.’

‘Maybe one of us should go ahead on foot to scout out the situation,’ said Nerlin.

‘OK, if you like,’ said Mordonna. ‘Off you go, Parsnip.’

‘Sky falling down. Snip-Snip cold,’ said the old bird as the clouds came down around them. ‘Need hot soup.’

‘You go and see what’s ahead. There’s a good boy,’ said Mordonna. ‘And when you get back I’ll give you a big mug of mulligatawny soup, with real tawny in it, your favourite.’

‘No prob, like, er, man. Snip-Snip go see wassup,’ said the bird, who had also got into the hippy thing.

He jumped down off the right-wing mirror and started walking up the track.

'What are you doing, you stupid bird?' Nerlin shouted after him.

'Snip-Snip go ahead on foot, like you said, man.'

'OK, OK. Well, there's been a change of plan,' said Nerlin. 'Go ahead on wing.'

'Right off, dude man,' said Parsnip and flew into the cloud.

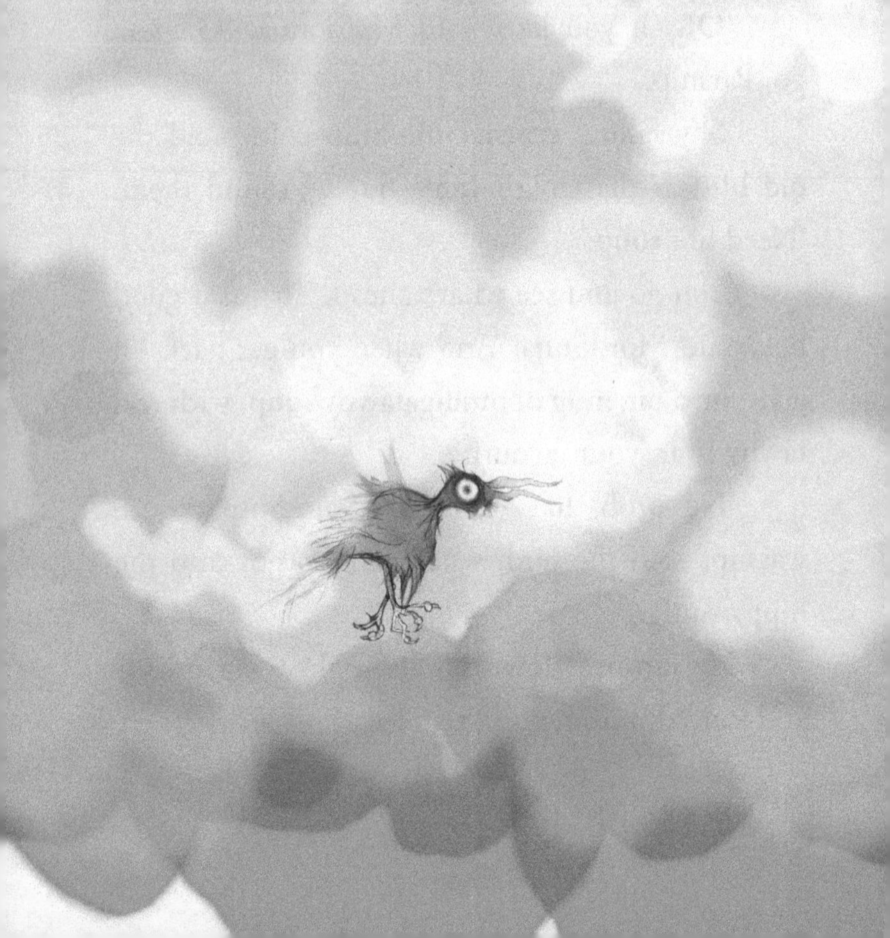

CHAPTER 2

Meanwhile, the Hulberts had arrived back at Acacia Avenue to find that the worst had indeed happened. The Floods' houses at numbers 11 and 13 had not simply been burnt to the ground, they had been blasted into total oblivion. There were no bits of brick wall or smouldering armchairs. There was just a very deep, black, still smoking hole. The whole site was cordoned off with that black and yellow keep-out tape and a team of policemen and forensic scientists were digging up the garden.

The trouble was that the blast had disturbed some of the Floods' relatives who had been

buried there. Great-Aunt Blodwen's knees had gone flying through the bedroom window of a house across the street and Uncle Flatulence's rib cage had trapped a small child who happened to be walking by at the time. Cousin Vein, who had only been half dead when he had been buried, was now wholly dead and mixed up in the branches

of a big tree, from where he was dripping onto an ambulance.

So now the police were treating the whole thing as a murder investigation.

'Well, I always said they were a strange family,' said the man who had woken up to find bits of Great-Aunt Blodwen in bed beside him. He was standing in the middle of the street with the rest of the neighbours, trying to see past the keep-out tape.

'So did I,' said his wife.

'But who would have thought they were mass murderers?' said the man.

'They killed my cat,' said the man's daughter.

'No they didn't,' said his wife. 'It was run over by a car. The Floods just ate it.'

'Don't be ridiculous,' said Mrs Hulbert. The Hulberts had arrived in their small rental car just as the road was blocked off by the police, so they were standing with the rest of the neighbours.

A creepy woman with a hat pulled down over her face and a very large pair of dark glasses came over to the Hulberts. She was holding a pencil and a notebook. It was the Hearse Whisperer.

'Excuse me,' she said. 'I am from the *Morning Herald*. Can I ask you a few questions?'

'Oh, er, um, we were away on holiday when this happened so we don't know anything,' said Mr Hulbert.

'Really, where?'

Fortunately, Winchflat, being a genius, had suspected the Hearse Whisperer might hang around looking for clues, so he had made each of the Hulberts a miniature Hearse-Whisperer-Warning-Device and implanted them under their armpits. If the Hearse Whisperer approached them the warning devices would start to tingle.

They were tingling like mad.

'Monte Carlo,' said Mr Hulbert at exactly the same time as Mrs Hulbert said, 'Las Vegas,' and Ffiona said, 'Paris.'

'We've been on a tour,' said Mr Hulbert.

'Blooga, blooga, amphibious,' said the baby Hulbert, Claude.

The Hearse Whisperer could tell they were lying, but she also knew that Mordonna must have inoculated each of them so that no matter what she did, they would never be able to tell her the truth even if they wanted to.

'So you didn't know the people who lived in the bombed houses then,' she said.

'No,' said Mr and Mrs Hulbert.

'How do you know it was a bomb?' said Ffiona. 'It could have been a gas leak.'

'Or a lightning strike,' said Mr Hulbert.

'Or someone left the gas on,' said Mrs Hulbert. 'And no, we did not know the Frauds.'

'The Frauds?' said the Hearse Whisperer.

'Wasn't that their name?' said Mrs Hulbert.

'Blooga, blooga, lighthouse,' said Claude.

'Well, little girl,' said the Hearse Whisperer, turning to Ffiona to try one last time to get the information she needed, 'did you have a lovely time at, um, where was it you said you'd been?'

'Scotland.'

'Excuse me,' said the Hearse Whisperer. She walked over to a large tree and banged her head against it.

Because it was the evil Hearse Whisperer doing this and not an ordinary person, the tree came off the worst. All its leaves shrivelled up and died and several of its larger branches came crashing down, squashing a cat that was just about to leap on a small bird, and totally wrecking a police car.

Which just goes to show, the Hearse Whisperer thought as she left, *that every cloud has a silver lining. Or in this case, two silver linings.*

'Snip-Snip bring love and peas, man,' said Parsnip when he arrived back at the Floods campervan an hour later.

'So it's hippies,' said Nerlin, 'and not a top secret military base.'

'Chill out, wizardman,' said Parsnip. 'Isallcool.'

They drove along the track, stopping to clear the rocks that had obviously been put there deliberately. Some of the rocks were so big it must have taken at least a dozen people to push them into place. Of course, for wizards, moving them

wasn't a problem. Each of them took it in turns transforming a rock into the vegetable of their choice. Everyone agreed that Betty's two-metre-tall cabbage was the best because when they drove the van into it, it rolled off down the road like a huge rolling cabbage.

The final obstacle on the road to Nowhere was a three-metre-wide ditch that had been dug across the road, but all it took to fill it in was a very small earthquake.

After that everything changed. They drove round a corner and the road began to go downhill. The clouds cleared and grass began to appear, then bushes then trees, then birds and softer, greener grass and softer, greener bushes and prettier birds until they found themselves in the most beautiful valley they had ever seen. It was the floor of a long-dead volcano, hidden away from the outside world like an enchanted place out of a fairy story.

Except for the scruffy old hippy who was standing right in front of their van.

He was smiling and holding out his open

hands in a love and peace sort of way, which usually means, 'Give me a piece of everything you've got and I will love you.'

'Welcome to Nowhere, man,' he said. 'I am Nameless.'

'Nameless?' said Mordonna.

'Yeah, man. I am Nameless because names are like possessions, they cage you. So when we all came here, we left our names out there.'

'How many of you are there?' said Nerlin.

'Thirty-seven, though we are one, man,' said Nameless.

'Including the women?' said Mordonna.

'What?'

'And you're all called Nameless?'

'Yeah, man.'

'So how do you know who is who?' said Mordonna.

'Yeah, well, man, no one said it was easy being, like, alternative,' said Nameless.

'So absolutely everyone here is called Nameless?'

'Oh, no, man,' said Nameless. 'The Cool One is not called Nameless. He's called Sanguine. He's like, our guru.'

'What about your animals?' asked Betty. 'Are they called Nameless too?'

'No, man. The dogs are all called Dog and the cats are all called Cat, though the Cool One is thinking of changing their names because he says it's, like, stereotyping.'

'So I suppose the chickens are all called Chicken?' said Betty.

'No.'

'What are they called then?'

'Ethel.'

'What, all of them?'

'Yeah.'

'OK,' said Mordonna. 'Moving on. Can we, like, chill here for a while?'

By now there were about fifteen Namelesses all gathered round. They nodded and did a bit of chanting and then said, 'Sure, man.'

'And remember,' said one of the Namelesses, who may or may not have been the same one they had been talking to earlier, 'there is, like, only one rule here and that is that there are no rules.'

'So where can we park?' said Winchflat.

'Oh, like, anywhere, man,' said Nameless.

'Well, I say anywhere and that's cool, but don't park over there by the orange yurt because that's, like, where the Cool One lives and he needs his space. And, like, down there is the Stamping Ground and that needs a lot of space for everyone to stamp. Same for the Sacred Chanting Place over there. And not under that tree, man, because there's a magpie's nest there and she's got, like, eggs and stuff so she needs her space. And not up there because that's, like, the Vegie Garden and, like, vegetables need their space too, man.'

'So how about over there by the fence?'

'Yeah, that's kind of cool, though of course the fence needs its space, man.'

'OK, where then?'

'Well, like, right where you are is cool.'

'If you are all so free,' said Betty, 'why do you have a fence? It's not as if there's any way to get in or out of the valley except by the track we came on and the fence doesn't actually fence anything.'

'Well, you might see it as a fence,' Nameless began.

'Because it is,' said Betty.

'No, but to us, it's, like, a symbol of the outside world where everyone is fenced in by authority and rules and stuff,' another Nameless finished.

'Yeah, no rules, no rules,' the others chanted over and over again until one of them pointed out it was five past six and they were all late for the Six O'Clock Chant.

'Like, the Cool One gets totally freaked if anyone is late for the Six O'Clock Chant,' said Nameless.

'But I thought you said there were no rules?' said Betty.

'No, there aren't, man,' said a Nameless.

'Except the Six O'Clock Chant rule,' said another.

'And the Eight O'Clock Chant rule,' said another.

'And the Midnight Chant rule,' said another.

'Yeah, man, and of course the Dawn Chant rule,' said another. 'Which is actually around ten o'clock in the morning because the Cool One says doing anything before then is, like, totally playing into the brainwashed work ethic thing.'

'And the three daily Stamping Rules.'

'And the Earwax Rule.'

'Don't ask,' said Mordonna, putting her hand over Betty's mouth.

'So you're saying,' said Winchflat, 'that there are no rules unless the Cool One makes one up.'

'Well, no, man, because the Cool One doesn't make up rules. He just leads us along the path to Nirvana with his, like, extreme wisdom and guiding hand.'

'I bet he never does the washing up, does he?' said Mordonna.

'Well, no, of course not, man. That is a great honour awarded to all the chicks.'

'What's washing up, man?' said another Nameless as they ran off to chant.

Nerlin drove the van well away from the rest of the old vans, buses, yurts, assorted containers, sheds and tents and parked under the shade of a huge old tree.

'I expect it's not good to park here. All those dead leaves in the grass probably need their space,' said Valla and they all fell about laughing.

'Are we actually going to stay here?' said Betty. 'They're a bunch of complete idiots.'

'I know that, sweetheart,' said Mordonna. 'But this is probably the best place to hide while we work out what to do. The Hearse Whisperer would never suspect for a second that we'd be in a place like this.'

A dreadful wailing noise drifted down the valley as the Six O'Clock Chant reached its peak. It sounded as if every single one of the thirty-seven hippies was chanting in a different key. The cats and dogs ran for shelter. The chickens, although they had heard the chants dozens of times, all did their best to fly up into the safety of the nearest tree.[7]

---

[7] *As everyone knows, the words 'chicken' and 'flying' don't really belong in the same sentence. So every time the hippies chanted, all the chickens crashed into the trees, losing feathers, dropping eggs everywhere and getting sore heads.*

'No wonder the cats are running away,' said Winchflat. 'That noise sounds like ten cats being strangled.'

'I wonder if they've got a manager,' said Satanella. 'I reckon every witches' coven in the galaxy would buy a CD of that, if only to keep evil spirits from running away.'

'Nevertheless,' said Mordonna, 'these strange people could be very useful.'

'You have a plan?' said Nerlin.

'Several.'

It was dark by then, which meant none of the hippies could see what the Floods were doing. So they collected seventeen sticks, three paper bags, four gold rings and a partridge in a pear tree in a pile next to the van. Mordonna got out her best wand – not the one she used every day for boiling kettles and getting rid of spots, but her special occasion wand – and, with a couple of spells, she turned the pile into several bedrooms, a kitchen and the only bathroom in the valley.

The chanting stopped and the Floods

watched the group of flickering lights disperse as the Namelesses went back to their vans, tents and yurty things.

'Thank goodness that's over,' said Nerlin.

'Mind you,' said Valla, 'the vibrations have loosened my earwax a treat.'

As the family all sat round cleaning out their ears with blunt sticks,[8] Nameless came up to them.

'OK, like, people, the Cool One has summoned you into his Aura,' he said to Mordonna.

'Really?'

'Yeah, it's, like, a seriously awesome invitation.'

'Oh yes?'

'Yeah, man. I mean, not everyone gets summoned into the Aura,' said Nameless. 'I've never been there.'

---

[8] *Don't try this at home. Actually, don't try it anywhere – especially in the back of a fast-moving vehicle on a bumpy road like my Uncle Frank did. We never did get every last bit of his brains out of the upholstery.*

'So much for you all rejecting the petty privileged class system of the outside world,' said Mordonna. 'Now you go and tell your so-called Cool One that if he wants to see me, he can come here.'

'Oh, no, man, I can't possibly do that,' said Nameless, obviously terrified at the prospect.

'Why not?'

'The Cool One never comes out of the Aura Area.'

'What, never?'

'No.'

'So none of you have ever even seen him?'

'No.'

'Do you mean that he never sets foot outside his yurt?' said Betty.

'Oh no,' said Nameless. 'He comes out quite often.'

'So you have all seen him then?'

'No, he comes out wearing his floating yurt,' said Nameless. 'It's like a personal tent that covers him from head to foot. Though my sister Nameless says that once, when she was lying on the grass in the pose of the dandelion, she saw one of his toes.'

'I wonder why he won't let anyone see him,' said Betty. 'I bet he's really ugly.'

'No, he says his aura is, like, so bright that if any of us saw it, it would strike us, like, totally blind.'

'Yeah, right,' said Betty.

'Well, off you go and give him my message,' said Mordonna.

'No, I can't,' Nameless whimpered. 'Please don't make me.'

'I thought you were supposed to be a community of free spirits with no rules and no one telling you what to do and everyone being equal?'

'Yeah, we, like, totally are.'

'Are you sure?'

'Oh, yeah, man, the Cool One tells us that.'

'Do you know what a dictatorship is?' Mordonna asked.

Nameless had no answer to that so Mordonna clicked her fingers and performed a bravery spell and sent Nameless off to the Cool One with her message.

Obviously the Cool One was not happy with the message because the air around his orange yurt turned purple and Nameless came running back.

'I, er, I, er, I, er . . .' was all he could say.

'It's all right,' said Mordonna. 'Just relax.'

'The Cool One is furious. He says if you don't go into his Aura, like, immediately, he will perform the Stamping On Uncool Ones Dance and make you leave Nowhere.'

'Really?' said Mordonna. 'We'll see about that. Come on, everyone, let's go and sort this Cool One out.'

So Mordonna, Nerlin, Queen Scratchrot, the seven children and Mildred Flambard-Flood went and stood in a row outside the orange yurt. Mordonna put her forefinger on her forehead and concentrated until she knew everything there was to know about the Cool One.

'Barry Trubshaw, come out here right now,' she called in a voice that was loud enough for the Cool One to hear, but not the Namelesses, who were too scared to come any closer than ten metres from the orange yurt.

A single very long swear word came out of the yurt, followed by silence.

'Barry Trubshaw, if you do not come out right now, I will begin to shout and all of your so-called followers will hear every word,' Mordonna continued.

'Shan't.'

'Last chance.'

'Go away. I, the Cool One, order you to go away right now.'

'You are not the Cool One. You are not even the slightest bit cool,' said Mordonna. 'You are Barry Trubshaw, a forty-five-year-old filing clerk who lost his job for stealing paperclips and whose hobby is collecting Belgian postage stamps. And if you don't come out here this instant, I will say all that very loudly so everyone in Nowhere can hear me. And, Barry Trubshaw, I will fetch your mother.'

Muttering and scuffling and more muttering came out of the darkness, followed by a short, overweight, balding middle-aged man in a dirty vest and even dirtier shorts.

The Cool One was about as cool as a freshly laid cowpat.

His moustache made him as cool as a freshly laid cowpat that had just been stood in by the cow that had been following the one that had made it.

The final touch was the plastic Star Trek medallion round his neck, which made him as cool as a freshly laid cowpat that had just been stood in by a lot of cows and was now covered in a swarm of hungry flies.[9]

'Keep your voice down,' said Barry Trubshaw, moving back into the shadows.

'OK,' said Mordonna. 'Here is the deal. You are going to help me and I am going to help you.'

'OK, OK, can we just talk inside?' said Barry Trubshaw, stepping further back into the darkness.

'No problem,' said Mordonna, following him into the yurt.

---

[9] *The flies were the bright orange ones you only ever see on fresh cowpats, which coincidentally were exactly the same shade of orange as the Cool One's yurt.*

CHAPTER 4

Meanwhile . . .

The Hearse Whisperer knew that the Hulberts knew the Flood family. She knew they knew that she knew and she also knew, or rather guessed, that Mordonna had protected them with a spell that she would not be able to break no matter how much magic or force she tried to use.

But the Hulberts were the only clue she had to the whereabouts of the Floods.

So while the Hulberts slept, she transformed herself into a cockroach, her favourite disguise. She slipped under the front door of their house

and took samples of dirt from under all of their fingernails. To do this she had to transform herself into a small monkey because cockroaches, although gorgeous, are rubbish at sample collecting. They simply can't undo the top of the sample collecting jar.

Baby Claude Hulbert woke up while the Hearse Whisperer was digging under his fingernails. Seeing a small furry animal in front of him, he grabbed it. For the next hour he cuddled the Hearse Whisperer tight, gurgling happily to himself until he finally fell asleep again. Incredibly, the Hearse Whisperer had found herself in exactly the same situation before. On those other occasions she had simply fried the little gurglers to a crisp and eaten them. This time, however, she suspected, quite rightly, that if she fried baby Claude something similar could well happen to her. She was sure that Mordonna would have protected the Hulberts with some sort of Back-At-You-Spell so anything she did to any of them would be done to her too. To test the theory she

made a pimple appear on Claude's bottom. Sure enough, not one but ten pimples popped up on her own.[10]

So she lay there for an hour being gurgled at and fighting a terrible urge to turn herself into a really prickly hedgehog. Then she slipped out of Claude's arms, carried her samples downstairs, changed back into her almost human form and quietly slipped out of the house.

As devious and clever as the Hearse Whisperer was, Winchflat Flood was cleverer. His Hulbert-Sensing-Device told him that the combined weight of the Hulbert family had decreased by 0.002 grams at a

---

[10] *The Hearse Whisperer had just been on an Anger Management course, but that hadn't really helped stop her hurting baby Claude since she had ended up eating the Anger Management consultant.*

time when they were fast asleep and therefore not going to the toilet or sweating.[11]

'The Hearse Whisperer has just collected samples from the Hulberts,' he reported. 'Just as I thought she would.'

In the secrecy of her room back at the Happy Traveller Motel, the Hearse Whisperer fed the samples into her ultra-miniature super-computer. It told her that the Hulberts had been on holiday and it told her where.

Port Folio.

[11] *Of course, being a toddler, baby Claude frequently went to the toilet when he was asleep, but that weighed a lot more than 0.002 grams.*

It analysed a minute speck of bacon and told her that they had stayed at the Hotel Splendide.

'Thank you, computer,' said the Hearse Whisperer. 'Of course, I had worked all this out myself, but it's useful to have you to confirm my findings.'

'Yeah, right,' said the computer.

'I did.'

'So what do you need me for, then?' said the computer, using Voice No. 4 (Grumpy).

'Well, I don't, actually . . .' the Hearse Whisperer began to say.

'OK then,' the computer interrupted and totally shut down.

This happened every single time the Hearse Whisperer used the computer. She simply could not handle the fact that a machine small enough to fit in her pocket could do stuff that she couldn't. And the computer couldn't handle the Hearse Whisperer's complete lack of respect for her awesome powers and always powered down in a huge sulk.

Then the Hearse Whisperer had to find the install disc and spend an hour coaxing and apologising to make the computer boot up again. The Hearse Whisperer didn't do apologising very well and always ended up in a really bad mood, which meant she then had to go out and hurt some poor innocent human or animal to make herself feel better.[12]

The Hearse Whisperer checked into the Hotel Splendide under the name of Henrietta

---

12 *Her favourite nasty thing was to make all the feathers fall out of a passing pigeon so that it (a) crashed, and (b) caught a cold. Melting all the cheese on every pizza in the largest supermarket so it ran all over the floor, causing lots of old ladies to break their ankles and massive shopping trolley gridlocks, came a close second.*

Widdenshaw – because, as everyone knows, if you ever use a false name it has to have the same initials as your real name. This is an International Law that even creatures as vile as the Hearse Whisperer always obey.

It took her less than five seconds to sniff out that the Hulberts and the Floods had been there. Their scent was everywhere. Now all she had to do was follow the scents out of the hotel and see where they had gone. This took a lot longer. She followed the scent of the two families all over the beach, in and out of the theatre and even round to the council dog pound, but all the trails just ended up back at the hotel.

At last, she got lucky. She followed Valla's scent to the graveyard and to the tomb of Mildred Flambard. As she sat on the heavy stone lid, her eye spied something that was almost trodden into the mud in one of Valla's footprints. Apart from one tiny corner it had been completely buried. She reached down and retrieved it.

It was a scrap of paper.

'They think they are so clever, those Floods,' she laughed to herself and to two bored bats that were hanging on a branch above her. 'But they always leave a clue.'

It was true. The Floods had previously managed to trap the Hearse Whisperer in a magic bottle and bury that bottle at the bottom of the deepest ocean[13] until an earthquake had set her free. They had been careless then and left an envelope attached to the bottle that had led the Hearse Whisperer to Acacia Avenue.

Now they had done it again.

'Amateurs,' sneered the Hearse Whisperer.

She smoothed the scrap of paper out on the top of Mildred Flambard's tomb. It was a flimsy copy from a credit card transaction, and although the mud and rain had washed away a lot of the information, there was enough left to see that it was Mordonna Flood's credit card and she had used it to buy ten first-class steamer tickets to Tristan da Cunha.

---

[13] *See* The Floods 5: Prime Suspect.

'Oh, not there again!' she said. 'How obvious to hide in the most remote place on earth.'

Because it is the most remote place on earth, Tristan da Cunha is also one of the most difficult to reach. It would be weeks before any ship the Floods had escaped on would reach the place. When they did, the Hearse Whisperer would be waiting for them. She would fly there – something the Floods could not do because, no matter what birds they transformed themselves into, Betty Flood and the twins were too young to make such a long journey. That was why they were travelling by sea.

Every time witches or wizards transform themselves into another life form it drains away some of their power. This is not like giving blood, where you always make more blood. The power they lose does not come back. So transformation is not something wizards do lightly. Some wizards never do it. Because of the nature of her job as a very evil secret agent and spy, however, the Hearse Whisperer had had to transform herself many, many times and the truth was that her terrible

powers, although still awesome, were down to about twenty per cent of their original strength.

She knew this. It was her fate. She lived to serve the Kings of Transylvania Waters and she knew that when her powers fell to below thirteen per cent it would be time to retire. Like so many spies before her, the Hearse Whisperer would spend the rest of her days as a chiropodist in the Street of a Thousand Chiropodists that clung to the West Wall of Castle Twilight.[14]

She already knew what her business slogan would be:

THE HEARSE WHISPERER
HORRIBLY HARD SKIN RIPPED AWAY WHILE YOU WAIT
No Pain $37 Extra

---

[14] *As will be revealed a bit later, the spies who ended up trimming people's infected toenails and verrucas for the rest of their lives were actually the lucky ones.*

A new Hearse Whisperer would be created and thus life, the universe and conspiracy would go on.

So she transformed herself into a giant albatross and soared up into the sky to catch a giant thermal[15] that would carry her to Tristan da Cunha.

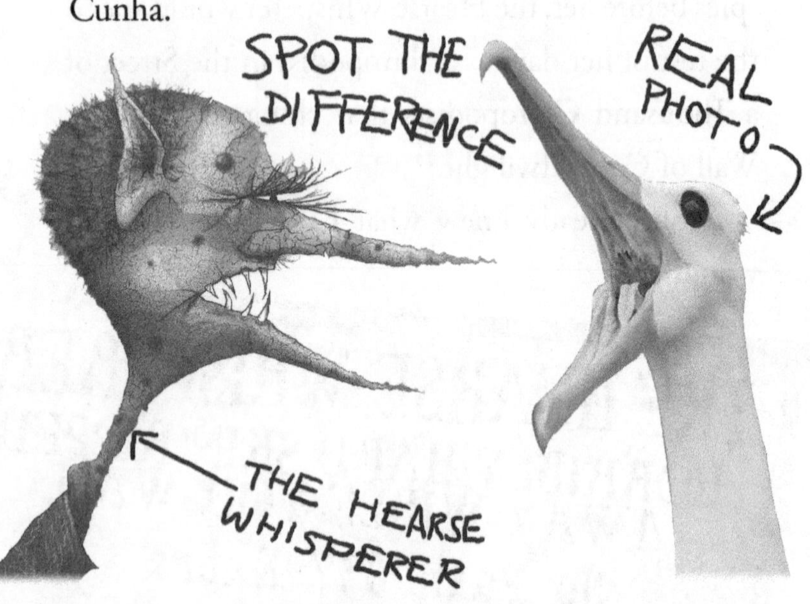

15 *Thermal as in thermal air current, not a thermal vest, though at such altitudes it was extremely cold and some warm clothing would have been very welcome. Scientific tests have shown, however, that huge sea birds cannot fly very well if you dress them in thermal underwear.*

'She has taken the bait,' said Winchflat as he pored over the dials of his Hearse-Whisperer-Detector,[16] 'and she is on her way to Tristan da Cunha.'

'Who would have thought it?' said Valla. 'I've really got to hand it to you, little brother. You are a genius.'

---

16 *This, of course, was not his original Hearse-Whisperer-Detector as that had been destroyed in the fire at Acacia Avenue. This was his Hearse-Whisperer-Detector Mark II, which was even more sensitive and could tell if the Hearse Whisperer had farted in an empty room up to 24 hours previously.*

'Indeed you are, my boy,' said Nerlin. 'I wish I had your brains.'

'I could make you a photocopy of them,' Winchflat offered.

'You'll do no such thing,' said Mordonna. 'Your father is perfect the way he is.'

Mordonna really meant it. She had fallen in love with Nerlin as he was and did not want him to change. And she most certainly did not like the idea of having a husband cleverer or even nearly as clever as she was.

'Just leave your father's brain alone,' she said. 'I have to go back and sort this Barry Trubshaw out.'

'Why bother?' said Betty. 'Why don't we just leave?'

'Because he is going to help us get Vessel back.'

She went back to the yurt, where she had left Barry Trubshaw in suspended animation when Betty had come over to tell her there was news about the Hearse Whisperer.

'OK,' Mordonna said to Barry now, clicking her fingers so he could move again, 'here is the deal. You are going to do one simple little thing for me and I am going to make you into everything you have been pretending to be.'

'What do you mean?' said Barry Trubshaw.

'I will make you tall, dark and handsome. I will give you charisma. I will clear all the rubbish out of your head and off your top lip and make you wise, sexy and seventeen years younger. In other words, I will make you into the Cool One – for real,' said Mordonna.

'Don't be ridiculous, you can't do that,' said Barry.

'Oh yes I can,' said Mordonna. 'I am a witch – not a tie-dyed-skirt-and-jangly-bells pretend witch, but a genuine witch with powers you have never dreamed of.'

'Come on,' said Barry. 'I wasn't born yesterday. There's no such thing as witches.'

'I'll prove it,' said Mordonna. 'What is the one thing you want more than anything in the world?'

Barry Trubshaw opened his mouth to speak, but before he could say a word, Mordonna held up her hand and said, 'The one thing you want more than anything in the whole world is something you are not even sure exists. The one thing you want more than anything in the whole world is a twelve-and-a-half-franc 1905 Belgian Mauve, a stamp so rare that no one has ever seen one in the flesh and the only proof it ever existed at all is one old faded photograph.'

Barry Trubshaw's mouth was still open but it was speechless. All he could do was give a feeble nod. As he did so it began to snow inside the yurt. Mauve snow drifted down in gentle flakes, appearing out of the darkness above them.

And every flake, all five thousand of them, was a genuine twelve-and-a-half-franc 1905 Belgian Mauve stamp.

'There you are,' said Mordonna. 'That is every Belgian Mauve stamp ever printed, the entire stock resurrected from the ashes of the Great Belgian Stamp Printing Works fire of 1905 that destroyed

them all the day before they were due to be released to the post offices of Belgium.'

Barry Trubshaw's mouth, still open, now made a noise. It whimpered.

'Of course, with five thousand of them, their legendary status and staggering value no longer exists,' said Mordonna. 'So I will now return four thousand, nine hundred and ninety-eight of them to the dust I collected them from, leaving you with two priceless treasures, one to keep and one to sell for an obscenely high price.'

Barry Trubshaw finally closed his mouth. He fell to his knees and tenderly picked up the two remaining stamps and placed them between the pages of his favourite book – an unpublished epic called *My Incredibly Brilliant and Exciting Life* by B. Trubshaw. Then he took them out again and placed them between the pages of his least favourite book – *My Son is a Twerp* by Mrs Trubshaw[17] – where they would be much safer.

---

[17] *Which had actually been published, though only in Belgium and Wales (so far).*

'What must I do, oh great and wonderful witch?' he said and he meant every word.

'Oh, nothing too difficult,' said Mordonna. 'You just have to go and collect an old birdcage.'

'Is there an old bird in the old birdcage?'

'There is, and he must be treated with the greatest care,' said Mordonna. 'For he is more than he seems, not so much an old bird as my mother's boyfriend under an evil spell.'

'Oh, right,' said Barry Trubshaw, wondering why someone as powerful as Mordonna could not go and get the cage herself.

'Will I, er, be in, like, danger?' he asked.

'No,' said Mordonna. 'Not really. Hardly at all. Just a bit.'

Barry Trubshaw began to wonder if two twelve-and-a-half-franc 1905 Belgian Mauves were such great things to have after all. If owning them carried a risk of getting dead, maybe he could live without them.

'You are wondering if two twelve-and-a-half-franc 1905 Belgian Mauves are such great things

to have after all, aren't you?' said Mordonna. 'Wondering if they are worth the risk of getting dead for?'

'Umm . . .'

'I'll tell you what,' said Mordonna. 'I'll do some of the other magic I promised you. I will make you a bit taller and cure your baldness and remove all those nasty blackheads from your back. When you bring the cage back here with the bird happy and safe inside, I'll do the dark and handsome bit and make you seventeen years younger. OK?'

Without waiting for his answer, Mordonna performed the spells. It was all a charade, really, because she could have simply taken her sunglasses off, stared deep into Barry Trubshaw's eyes and made him do whatever she wanted without all the stamp and image-changing stuff. But sometimes using magic was more fun and she realised that someone as pathetic as B. Trubshaw did not deserve the unbelievable joy of staring into her eyes.

'Stand up,' she commanded.

Barry Trubshaw stood up and bashed his head on the central beam across the middle of the yurt.

'See, I told you I'd make you taller,' said Mordonna. 'Now I am going to put a map inside your head of where you have to go. I will turn one of your chickens into a horse and one of your pumpkins into a packet of cheese and pickle sandwiches and a bottle of cordial, and you can set out on your quest.'

Barry Trubshaw rubbed the sore bit on top of his head and found that he was no longer bald. Where he had previously reflected moonlight, he now had a thick head of hair – a thick head of hair matted with blood from where he'd hit himself.

'Stamps beyond price, taller *and* hairy,' said Mordonna. 'Come on, off you go. And by the way, failure is not an option, as they say in the movies.'

'What would, er, happen if I failed?' Barry asked.

'Stamped *on*, much, much shorter, every single hair on your body removed with fire and when it

does grow back it will be bright ginger and you will only be able to speak an obscure language that only three very, very old people on a remote farm in Belgium can understand,' Mordonna said with a smile. 'But don't worry, you'll be fine. If there is anyone guarding the birdcage, just wait until they are asleep, get the cage and slip away without waking them. Just whisper my name to the old bird and he will understand.'

Barry Trubshaw climbed onto the horse, then climbed down and back on again so his head was facing the same direction as the horse's head. Then he got down and went to the toilet three times because the whole thing had made him very nervous, before climbing back up again and setting off along the valley towards the track back to the outside world.

'And remember,' Mordonna called after him, 'I will be watching you every step of the way, so no running home to Mummy and hiding in that secret place you made in the garden shed where you keep those magazines.'

'You entrusted that self-important fat little bald man with the task of rescuing my beloved Vessel?' cried the Queen.

'Yes, Mother, and I have no doubt he will bring him back here without any trouble at all,' said Mordonna. 'Barry will merely act as a robot that I can channel my powers through. Besides, the Hearse Whisperer is on her way to Tristan da Cunha and any guards she will have posted to look after Vessel's cage will be very lowly third-rate idiots who would never suspect a fifth-rate idiot like Barry Trubshaw. They'll just think he's some loony hippy roaming round the country on an old horse, which he is.'

Mordonna was absolutely right.[18] Barry Trubshaw rode through the forest until he came

---

18 *Which, of course, she ALWAYS is.*

to the deserted house where the Hearse Whisperer had trapped Vessel in the enchanted cage, and sure enough there were two third-rate idiots sitting outside on the verandah.

'I am so bored that if summink don't happen really soon,' said the first idiot, 'I fink I will die of boredom.'

'Yeah, well,' said the other idiot, 'I reckon I am so bored that I prob'ly already have died of boredom.'

'Hang on,' said idiot one, 'someone's coming.'

'Do me a favour, you say that every single day,' said idiot two. 'And you always say it at exactly seventeen minutes past four.'

'No, no, I mean it, someone really is coming.'

'You say that every day too.'

'I know, but no, I mean, I can hear a horse,' said idiot one.

'You aren't never said that before,' said idiot two.

'That's 'cos I din't never heard a horse before. Look, see, horse and man on horse.'

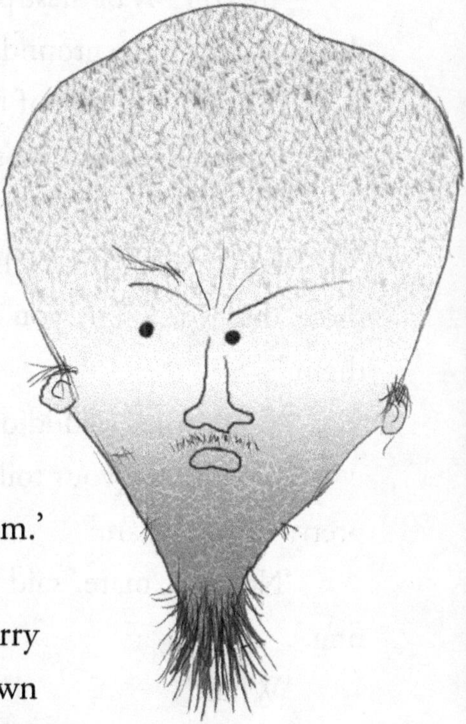

'It's a hippy,' said idiot two. 'Where's me gun?'

'I fink the guns rustid away wiv boredom.'

'Oh yeah.'

'Hi, man,' said Barry Trubshaw, climbing down from his horse. 'Can I use your toilet?'

'Hippy wants the toilet,' whispered idiot one to idiot two. 'That's all right, innit?'

'Yeah, course it is,' said idiot two, 'but we got to check him first.'

He opened a folder and took out a set of photos.

'Are you any of these peeps?' he said, spreading the pictures on the ground.

The pictures were of the Floods.

'Cause if you are, we're s'posed to kill you.'

''Cept our guns is broke.'

'Look, man,' Barry lied, 'I don't know who those dudes are, but you can see I'm not one of them.'

'That's true,' said idiot one.

'So can I use your toilet?' said Barry. 'It's, like, pretty urgent, man.'

'No prob, mate,' said idiot two. ''Cept for one fing.'

'What?'

'We aren't got no toilet.'

'You can use my bush,' said idiot one, pointing at an old gooseberry bush across the track.

'Or else you can use my bush,' said idiot two,

pointing at the gooseberry bush next to it.

So he wouldn't show any favouritism, Barry Trubshaw used both bushes.

'Do you two, like, live here on your own?' he asked.

'Yes,' said idiot one. 'There's me and him.'

'And the old bird,' said idiot two.

'What, you mean, like, your wife?'

'No, no, mate,' said idiot one. 'It's a bird. Like, it's got fevvers.'

'Yeah, it's in a cage,' added idiot two.

'Why?'

'Dunno, but we're s'posed to guard it. Stop anyone stealing it,' said idiot two. 'You wanna see?'

'Why on earth would anyone want to steal a scruffy old wreck like that?' said Barry Trubshaw when they took him inside and showed him Vessel's cage. 'Does it talk?'

'Yeah, it does, acherly,' said idiot one. 'It swears all the time.'

'Rude words,' idiot two giggled. 'Go on, do some rude words, birdie.'

Vessel let out a string of the filthiest curses and swear words that Barry Trubshaw had ever heard, followed by a lot more that he had never heard. The two idiots collapsed on the floor laughing, tears streaming from their eyes, doubled up with pain yet unable to stop.

Barry Trubshaw went closer to Vessel's cage and whispered, 'Mordonna sent me.'

Vessel fell off his perch.

'Hey, what you doin' to that bird?' said idiot one. 'Did you poke it?'

'No.'

'I reckon you poked it wiv a stick.'

'No I didn't.'

'So why did it fall off its perch?' said idiot two.

'Because I told it a swear word that it had never heard before,' said Barry.

'Really? Brilliant. Tell it to us.'

'Mackerel,' said Barry Trubshaw.

'That's disgusting,' idiot one giggled. 'Mack'rel, mack'rel, mack'rel.'

'Do another one,' said idiot two.

'Yeah, make the stupid bird fall off again.'

Barry went up close to Vessel's cage and winked at him. Vessel winked back and when Barry said, 'Organiser', he let out a squawk and fell off his perch.

'Organwossit, that's really rude,' idiot two sniggered and the two of them fell on the floor laughing again.

By the time midnight arrived and everyone was ready to fall asleep, Barry Trubshaw had the two idiots eating out of the palm of his hand. He did this by putting bits of his cheese and pickle sandwiches in his palm and holding it out to them. All the two guards had had to eat for the past few years had been stinging nettle soup and boiled gooseberries, which, considering what they used the gooseberry bushes for, didn't taste too good.[19]

'Would you do us a big favour?' said idiot one.

'Of course I will,' said Barry Trubshaw. 'I am your friend and that's what friends are for.'

'Would you sleep in wiv de old bird?'

'Sure, why?'

'Well, our boss said we was never to let it out

---

[19] *If you have ever been forced to eat gooseberries, you will realise that they taste awful even if the bushes haven't been used as a toilet. They are disgusting. They look like nasty spiny sea creatures, but don't taste as nice as nasty spiny sea creatures. I was also going to say that the two idiots had been using nettles instead of toilet paper, but the very thought of it made my eyes water so much that I couldn't even type the right words.*

of our sight so we've had to sleep down here on the floor every night while there is two really comfuble beds upstairs,' idiot two explained.

'Why didn't you bring the beds down here?' said Barry.

'Couldn't do that,' said idiot one. 'Beds goes in bedrooms. This is a lounge room.'

'Well, how about, and this is only a suggestion,' Barry said, 'how about taking the birdcage upstairs every night?'

'Oh,' said idiot two.

'You're brilliant, you are,' said idiot one. 'You give us sammiches, two new swear words and a way that we can sleep in the comfuble beds *and* watch the old bird.'

He put his arms round Barry Trubshaw and told him that he was their best friend and he would like Barry to stay with them forever.

'What a great idea,' said Barry. 'But I will sleep downstairs with the bird tonight, so you can have a really good sleep without being woken up by all the swearing at dawn.'

'You're brilliant, you are,' said idiot two, hugging Barry as well.

'Tell you what I'll do as well,' said Barry.

'Got more sammich?'

'No, better.'

'More swear words.'

'No, better.'

'What, what, what?'

'Bedtime story.'

'See, I told you,' said idiot two. 'We *have* died of boredom, but now we gone to hevun.'

Along with a Barry-Trubshaw-Tracking-Device, Mordonna had implanted a magic hypnotising bedtime story inside Barry Trubshaw's brain. A story that made anyone who heard it fall into a deep, deep sleep. Assuring them that Vessel would be fine left on his own for a little while, Barry took the two idiots upstairs, tucked them up in bed, having first cleared out the mice, the cockroaches and the mould that had spent the past two years living in the beds while the idiots had slept on the floor downstairs. Then he told them

the bedtime story, and within one hundred and thirteen seconds the two guards were fast asleep. Which is to say, they were *slow* asleep, because their breathing slowed right down and their hearts barely ticked over as they fell into such a deep hibernation that it would be spring before they woke up again.

Five minutes later Barry Trubshaw was riding away into the forest with Vessel's cage held firmly between his knees.

The Hearse Whisperer had passed several ships as she flew on towards Tristan da Cunha. The Floods could have been on any one of them or even, she thought, split up and each travelling on a different ship. But it was far simpler for her to go straight to the island and wait for them to arrive than to fly down and search each ship. Also, that would have meant transforming herself twice for each ship she landed on and she really needed to keep her transformations to a minimum.[20]

---

20 *Every evil spy is plagued with nightmares of doing their last*

Plenty of time, she thought, *to come up with a nice welcome. Something they will never forget.*

Of course, they wouldn't have to remember it for very long, because, apart from Mordonna, who the Hearse Whisperer would take back to her father in Transylvania Waters, the rest of them would be dead. So her wonderful welcome would be the very last thought in their heads.

Well, actually, she thought, *my little welcome ceremony will be the thought before the last thought*

---

transformation and losing their final bit of magic. It would mean that whatever form they were in when the very last transformation happened would be how they looked for the rest of their lives. As her magic faded, the Hearse Whisperer had these bad dreams almost every day and each one was worse than the one before. In the latest one she was a junior prune taster in the court of Henry VIII, not even the chief prune taster. The trick was to retire to the Street of a Thousand Chiropodists before you reached the very last transformation. The Hearse Whisperer did not want to end up like her great-grandmother, who was now a large black slug living on a cabbage in the kitchen garden of a deserted Belgian monastery. No, if she timed it right, she could spent the rest of her life working at the House of Corns. Though when she thought about it, maybe being a cabbage in a deserted monastery was not such a bad option.

in their heads. The very last thought will be something along the lines of 'Ahhhhhh, I am dea . . .'

The Hearse Whisperer laughed so much, she nearly collided with a Boeing 747.

'So actually,' she said to herself, 'they *will* forget, because they'll all be dead. And as my old grandmother used to say, "Dead men don't keep diaries."'

This made her laugh even harder and almost sent her crashing down into the sea.

'Hello, sweetheart. I haven't seen you in these parts before,' said a male albatross, drifting across to her as she got her balance again. 'You're an exceptionally gorgeous young lady.'

'Have you heard of fried chicken?' snarled the Hearse Whisperer.

'No, darling. What's that then?' said the albatross. 'My name's Albert, by the way. Albert Ross. What's yours?'

'Death,' said the Hearse Whisperer, turning him into the thing he hadn't heard of. 'And this is a fried chicken.'

Considering they were out of sight of land in every direction, it was amazing that Albert, the fried chicken, did not land in the sea. He plummeted down towards the sea, but just as he was about to dive into it, a ship got in the way and he landed on someone's head.

'That,' said the captain, looking down onto the deck where the ship's nurse was giving mouth-to-mouth resuscitation plus a little salt and pepper to a child with a roast chicken stuck on its head, 'is not something you see every day.'

The rest of the journey to Tristan da Cunha was fairly uneventful apart from a close encounter with a UFO, which the Hearse Whisperer programmed

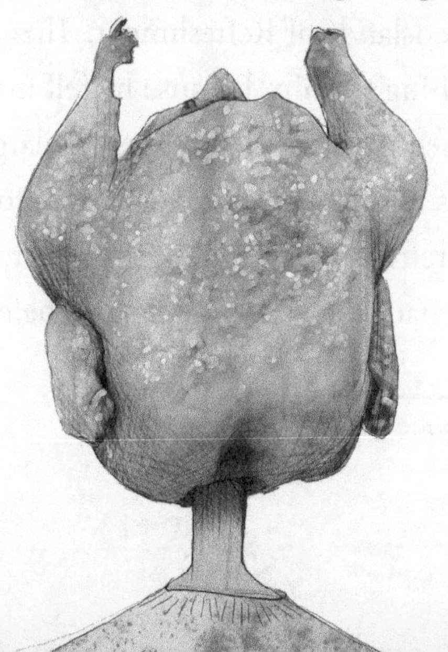

herself to forget about because she knew no one would believe it, and nearly colliding with some bearded millionaire racing round the world in a hot-air balloon.

Tristan da Cunha is the most remote place on earth. It is the tip of an almost, but not quite, extinct volcano and is home to around two hundred and seventy-five people. If it did not really exist, it would have had to have been made up.[21] It was named in 1506 by an explorer who was the first human to see it. Even though he didn't actually land on the island, he still named it after himself. In 1810 an American became the first person to go and live there, and he renamed the group of islands The Islands of Refreshment. They were not very refreshing for him because he fell into the sea and drowned two years later. The very large lobster that ate his remains is reported to have found him extremely refreshing. Incredibly, the current Island Governor had worked in Belgium before being

---

21 *Like Belgium was.*

promoted to look after the most remote place on Earth.

The Hearse Whisperer landed on the rim of the sleeping volcano, transformed back into her own body and looked down over the small town. It would be four weeks at the very least before the Floods would arrive by sea. She could have a holiday.

'A holiday?' she said to herself. 'Now I know I am getting old. I don't do holidays. I do spying and killing and pain.'

'And I don't do talking to myself,' she added.

'Now I am depressed,' she said out loud.

'You're depressed? You're depressed?' said a rat that had crawled out from under a stone. 'What do you have to be depressed about? You can leave here whenever you want. Just turn into that big bird again, fall off that rock and soar away over the horizon to somewhere else and a bright new tomorrow.'

The Hearse Whisperer liked rats as much as she liked anything. They lived in disgusting places and

carried all sorts of awful diseases like the bubonic plague. They were her kind of animal.

'There is a somewhere else over the horizon, isn't there?' said the rat. 'This island isn't the whole world, is it?'

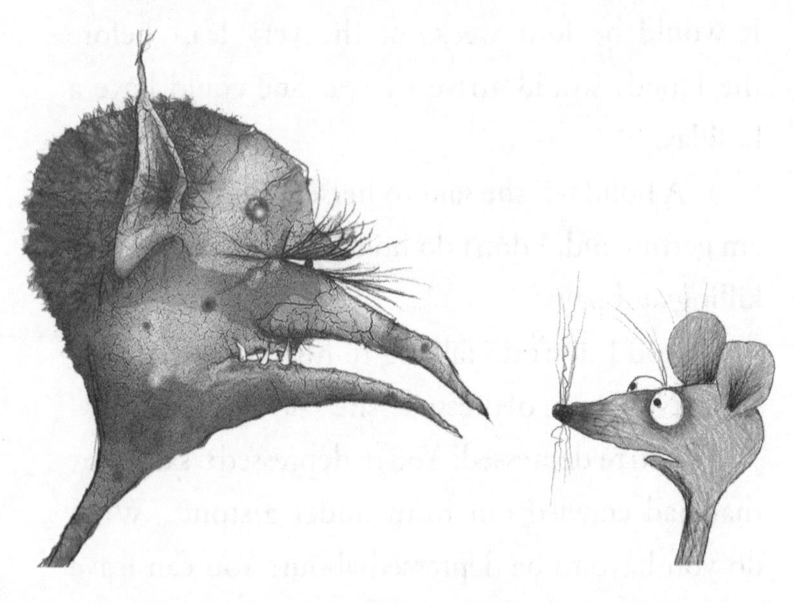

'No, there's millions of other places and nearly all of them are a lot bigger than here,' said the Hearse Whisperer.

'And do the humans in all these other places try to kill every rat they see like they do here?'

'Well, yes, actually they do.'

'Now I'm even more depressed,' said the rat. 'I was going to ask you to take me with you when you go, but there doesn't seem much point. I might as well stay here and take my chances with the other rats on annual Ratting Day.'[22]

The Hearse Whisperer had come to the conclusion that Tristan da Cunha rats were not cool harbingers of doom and destruction like rats everywhere else, but whingeing, boring creatures who thought the wickedest thing they could do was bite a potato.

If I had my way, she thought, *every day would be Ratting Day*.

'See that little hole down there with the volcanic steam slipping out from underneath it,' she said, pointing down into the sleeping volcano. 'Did you know that it is a magic time-warp gate that leads to another world?'

---

22 *On a small island like Tristan da Cunha rats are unwelcome visitors, so once a year they have a Ratting Day when they try to catch as many as they can. There are prizes, including one for the longest rat tail!*

'Wow, that's amazing,' said the rat. 'So if I go down there I'll be transported away from here and into a bright new tomorrow?'

'Oh yes,' said the Hearse Whisperer. 'I promise you that if you go down that hole, your future will be very bright indeed.'

Very short, but very, very bright, she thought.

'Brilliant,' said the rat and ran down into the volcano.

'BYE!' he shouted back up to the Hearse Whisperer.

'Whatever.' She held her nose because she couldn't stand the smell of burning rat fur.

By an unbelievable fluke, the hole was not a vent from the seething fires at the centre of the Earth as the Hearse Whisperer had presumed, but a real time-warp gate to another world, one of only three on this planet.[23] Well, not so much to another world, as to another country. So the poor innocent rat was not frizzled into oblivion, but whooshed away from Tristan da Cunha to a small cobbled square somewhere in Belgium. Unfortunately, the rat only had about 2.4 seconds to start thinking, *Wow, this is brilliant*, before he was flattened by a tram.

The rat incident was the highlight of the Hearse Whisperer's four weeks' holiday on Tristan da Cunha.

---

[23] *The second one is at Quicklime College in Patagonia. The third one is top secret and actually never stays in the same place for more than a few minutes. Winchflat Flood, of course, has built a Time-Warp-Gate-Detector so he is the only person who always knows where it is. See* The Floods 8: Better Homes and Gardens – *which, strangely, I haven't even written yet!*

CHAPTER 7

'My beloved,' cried Queen Scratchrot, her eyes overflowing with tears of joy. 'Is that really you?'

Vessel, the Queen's true love, was still trapped inside the enchanted birdcage in the body of a crow, and as one crow pretty much looks like another crow, even to another crow, Queen Scratchrot could only hope that the scruffy black bird looking up at her was indeed her beloved Vessel and not some devious fake planted there by the Hearse Whisperer.

'Yes, my beloved, it is I, your true love and faithful servant,' said Vessel, who then spoilt the

romance of the moment by adding, 'Who's a pretty boy then?'

'Snip-Snip think you truly gorgeous hunk,' said Parsnip, who appreciated Vessel's fine coal-black plumage as only another crow could. 'Snip-Snip say you cool dude number one pretty boy.'

'Can you return my true love to his old self?' the Queen asked Mordonna.

'Yes and no,' said Mordonna. 'First we must free him from the enchanted birdcage and to do that we must immerse it in the Terrible Pool of Vestor. Only that can dissolve the cage and set him free, and then I can return him to his previous form.'

'And talking of magic,' said Barry Trubshaw, 'what about your promise? When do I get to be tall, dark and handsome and all the other cool stuff?'

'I will make you tall,' said Mordonna. 'Stand up.'

Barry Trubshaw stood up and hit his head again.

'I will make you dark and handsome,' said Mordonna.

Barry Trubshaw looked in the mirror and fell in love with himself.

'The charisma bit isn't so easy,' said Mordonna. 'I mean, you are still called Barry and no one called Barry can ever be cool. It's one of the basic laws of the universe.'

'No, no,' said Barry Trubshaw, 'I'm not Barry. I am Sanguine, the Cool One.'

'You are still Barry, though,' said Mordonna, 'no matter what you call yourself.'

'Couldn't you change my name?' said Barry.

'Oh yes, we could give you a new name,' said Mordonna. 'Here's one. It's dynamic, mysterious and a little exciting. You are now called Argon.'

'I like it,' said Barry, now totally unable to take his eyes off his reflection in the mirror.

'Well, actually, you are called Argon Barry, which is not cool, but I'll tell you what I can do,' Mordonna added. 'I'll give you a "du". You can be Argon duBarry.'

'Oh yeah baby, that is really cool,' he said. 'Good morning, I am Argon duBarry.'

'Aren't you just,' said Betty.

'No, no, listen. This is even better,' said Barry.

'*Bonjour, je suis* Argon duBarry.'

'The trouble is,' Mordonna continued, 'that, inside, you are still Barry Trubshaw. You are called Argon, but you will never truly *be* Argon. Still, don't worry about it. Compared to the weirdos you've collected here, even being plain Barry you're cooler than they are. It's all relative.'

'So have I got this charisma thing now?' said Barry Trubshaw.

'Compared to your followers you are super-sophisticated,' said Mordonna.

'Far out,' said Argon duBarry, not realising that his name now made him sound like a third-rate hairdresser.

'Far out indeed,' said Mordonna.

As the Floods packed up to leave, Argon duBarry Trubshaw Sanguine Cool One summoned his followers to the Stamping Ground.

'We will gather in half an hour,' he said from the darkness of his yurt.

'But it doesn't get dark for three hours, oh great master,' said Nameless.

'I know,' said Argon duBarry Trubshaw Sanguine Cool One. 'The time has come for me to expose myself to you all.'

Some of the younger Namelesses giggled.

'So much for love and peace and all that Karma stuff,' said Mordonna as they drove off back down the track away from Nowhere. 'Time we went somewhere.'

The Hearse Whisperer was still waiting. She had sent seventeen rats, four mice and a shrew down the magic time gate to Belgium, where 35 per cent of them were now leading new and exciting lives while 65 per cent were being scraped off tram wheels.

Not long now, she thought, looking down into the volcano. *I'd better start preparing my surprise welcome.*

And then it began to snow.

CHAPTER 9

'Where are we going?' said Betty when they left the track from Nowhere and got back on the road.

'Well, obviously we have to go to the Terrible Pool of Vestor,' said the Queen. 'To remove the enchantment from my beloved Vessel.'

'F@@#XXX!!!!£,' swore Vessel, followed by, 'GR!!***&∞¢¢KK*! Mackerel, Mackerel, Mackerel F$$**!! Organiser!!!'

'That's enough of that,' said Mordonna. 'There are children present.'

'It was them I learnt the words from,' said Vessel.

'It's all right, Mum,' said Betty. 'They aren't real swear words. I just made them up.'

'Well, actually, F@@#XXX!!!!£ *is* a real swear word,' said Nerlin.

'Oh, cool, Dad,' said Betty. 'What does it mean?'

'You tell her and you're dead,' said Mordonna quick as a flash.

'OK, OK, we all know lots of rude words,' snapped the Queen, 'but are we going to the Terrible Pool of Vestor or not?'

'Of course we are, Mother,' said Mordonna.

'Where is it?' asked Nerlin, who was doing the driving and had spotted a particularly interesting tree with four sheep standing underneath it. 'Left, right, straight ahead, where?'

'Ah, well now, that's a question,' said Mordonna.

It was indeed a question, and it was a question that none of them knew the answer to.

'Another question we need to answer,' Mordonna continued, 'is how long do you think

we've got before the Hearse Whisperer realises we are not going to Tristan da Cunha?'

'About a week at most, I reckon,' said Winchflat. 'She is still there and I have made it snow really hard so she can't fly around to see if we're coming. So that'll give us a bit more time.'

'You are such a clever boy,' said Mordonna and Nerlin at the same time.

'Nah, nah, nah,' said Merlinmary. 'You are such a clever boy. Can't get a girlfriend, though, can you?'

'Merlinmary!' snapped Mordonna. 'You apologise this instant or I'll stick jump leads in your ears.'

'Sorry,' said Merlinmary.

'That's all right, fusewire face,' said Winchflat.

The twins giggled and prodded each other. Obviously everyone had been stuck together in the cramped van for too long and needed more space.

'Hey,' said Nerlin, 'we're supposed to be hippies, remember? That means we have to, like,

totally chill, man. Whatever that means.'

'Right, everyone, calm down,' said Mordonna. 'The obvious thing to do is look on Google Earth. Just type in the Terrible Pool of Vestor and we'll go there.'

Winchflat hunched over his laptop, tapping away and muttering to himself.

'Mmmm . . .'

'What?'

'Mmmm, yes, well, mmmmm.'

'What?'

'There appear to be six of them,' said Winchflat.

'*Six* Terrible Pools of Vestor?' said Mordonna. 'Are you sure your computer's working OK?'

'Yes.'

While this had been going on, Nerlin had been driving the van across the featureless moors, which were called 'moors' because there seemed to be more and more of them and 'featureless' due to the lack of features. Their overall colour was grey and their underall colour was grey too, mixed with grey.

This was a landscape for depression. If you were happy when you went there you would become depressed very quickly. This was a landscape where you expected to turn a corner and see a bleak grey house with a single weak light at one window. The house would be far back from the road, silhouetted against the evening sky. It would have one twisted tree and a big black dog whose only pleasure in life was howling with a sad, empty, eerie howl that curdled milk. It would be the sort of house where you would never know how many rooms there were or how many people lived there. Some of the people would be chained to the walls and live on water that dripped from the ceiling and slimy lizardy things.

'Oh, look,' said Betty, as they turned a corner, 'up that long winding track, silhouetted against the evening sky, a bleak grey house with a single weak light at one window.'

'How beautiful,' said Mordonna. 'Maybe they could put us up for the night.'

'Look at the really interesting tree,' said Nerlin.

'And listen to that wonderful dog singing so beautifully,' said Satanella. 'I bet he's really handsome with a voice like that.'

'I, er . . .' Mildred Flambard-Flood began.

'What's the matter, my dear?' said Mordonna. 'Surely you're not scared of such a beautiful place?'

'I am,' said Mildred. 'For I have been here before.'

'Are you sure?' said Valla.

'Oh yes,' said Mildred. 'Even though it was over two hundred years ago, I would not forget the place I died. Nor would I forget the mournful howl of Brastof, my faithful hound, chained to the wall

of the darkest dungeon where I spent my last days alive.'

'Are you saying that howling dog is the actual dog you left behind over two hundred years ago?' said Mordonna.

'Indeed,' said Mildred, 'and that place is Forsaken Hall, the home of the Knights Intolerant, whose sole aim in life was to destroy every wizard and every witch on the face of this earth.'

'I've heard of them,' said Queen Scratchrot. 'My grandfather used to talk about them when I was a child. He said they are the very reason Transylvania Waters exists. The wizards of old were hunted almost to extinction and the few remaining families fled into the darkest valleys of Eastern Europe to seek sanctuary and those valleys became Transylvania Waters. I always thought he made it all up to scare us into not being naughty.'

'Oh no,' said Mildred. 'They are real. I bear the marks to prove it.'

'But surely they would have died out long ago, wouldn't they?' said Betty.

'I'd have thought so,' said Mordonna. 'Otherwise we would have heard of them.'

'And what about the dog?' said Valla. 'If someone wasn't feeding it, wouldn't it have died a long time ago too?'

'Unless it's a ghost,' said Morbid. 'I mean, there's not many dogs live for over two hundred years.'

'Wow,' said Satanella, 'a ghost dog. How cool. I wonder if it's got a ghost rubber ball we can play with.'

As they drove up the track towards the house, the cold evening air got even colder. The puddles by the road that had been filled with water were now filled with ice and every blade of grass was frozen stiff with frost. Even with the campervan's heater on full, the cold reached into everyone's skin and made them shiver. Seven black crows flew out of the black clouds, circled the van and flew off blackly towards the house, where they vanished into the black shadows. And all the time mournful howling filled the air.

'I don't like this,' Mordonna. 'I think we should go back.'

'OK,' said Nerlin and stopped.

The track was very narrow and it took lots of backwards and forwards to turn it round.

'No, darling,' said Mordonna. 'You were supposed to say that it will be all right and reassure us all.'

'Except I think you're right,' said Nerlin. 'I don't like it either.'

'But we are the Floods – we don't run from anything,' said Mordonna.

'Except your father,' said Queen Scratchrot.

'Except my father,' Mordonna agreed.

'And the Hearse Whisperer,' Nerlin added.

'Yes, and the Hearse Whisperer.'

'And very big spiders,' said Betty.

'We don't run from very big spiders,' said Merlinmary.

'I do.'

'I don't,' said Merlinmary. 'I eat them.'

'All right, all right. We are the Floods and

we do not run away from many things and one of the things we never run away from are bleak grey houses with a single weak light at one window that are a long way from the road, silhouetted against the evening sky with one twisted tree and a big howling dog. We never run away from them.'

'Couldn't we make an exception this time?' said Nerlin.

'No,' said Mordonna. 'Turn around. We are going on.'

'Umm, can I just say something?' said Winchflat.

'Later, dear,' said Mordonna. 'Come on, husband, turn around. Not you, you idiot, the van.'

'But . . .' Nerlin began.

'But . . .' Winchflat began.

Mordonna clicked her fingers and the van lifted seven centimetres up off the track, its wheels still spinning. Then it turned one hundred and eighty degrees and dropped back onto the ground.

'We are going on,' said Mordonna.

Forsaken Hall was surrounded by a grey stone wall that had once been two metres tall and topped with steel spikes. Now the spikes had rusted away in the dampness of the mist that endlessly swirled around the place. It was this mist that meant most travellers along the main road never saw the house. It was not on any maps and this was not the sort of place passing drivers would say, 'Oh, look, a track. I wonder what's up there?' This bleak location was exactly why the Knights Intolerant had built their house there.

The wall had fallen down in places. The two huge gates had fallen over too, and it was only the single light in the window, a light that had gone out as soon as the Floods had begun to drive up the track, that indicated there might be someone living there. The windows were curtained in thousands of cobwebs.

They climbed out of the van and walked to the front door. It was open a few centimetres, though more cobwebs told them it had been that way for a long time.

'Hello?' Mordonna called.

Nothing.

'Hello?' she called louder.

Footsteps and muttering echoed inside the hall and the door slowly began to open.

'Hello, there. Great snow, isn't it?' said a penguin.

The Hearse Whisperer had been watching the penguin for three days. That was how long it had taken the poor bird to jump out of the sea, scramble over the rocks, waddle across the famous Tristan da Cunha Potato Patches and clamber up the slippery rocks to the top of the volcano. It had fallen down seventy-three times, but because it only had room inside its head for one thought at a time, and that thought was, *I am going up the mountain*, it kept trying over and over again until it finally made it.

'Don't be stupid,' said the Hearse Whisperer. 'Snow is disgusting stuff – all that pure cold whiteness.'

'But it's a great view, isn't it?' said the horribly cheerful little bird, whose head was now full of the thought that said, *Great view, isn't it?*

'It's rubbish,' said the Hearse Whisperer. 'Some rocks, a bit of grass and lots of sea. What's so great about that?'

'Well, why are you here then?' said the penguin.

'I'm waiting for someone.'

'Buried up to your neck in snow on the top of a volcano in the most remote place on earth and you're waiting for someone?' said the penguin. 'Do you not think that maybe – and this is just an idea – do you not think that this is probably the very last place you would ever meet them?'

The Hearse Whisperer turned to face the penguin and was just about to fry the poor innocent bird when a really, really large penny dropped. She could feel the veins inside her head begin to throb,

and when they did that she got really, really angry, as anything alive within a fairly large radius would discover very suddenly when the Hearse Whisperer converted them into a small pile of charcoal dust.

'Penguin,' she said between gritted teeth, 'I am deeply indebted to you so I have to tell you that you must leave here very, very quickly.'

'No probs,' said the penguin. 'I only came up here so I could slide all the way down the ice on my tummy and shoot off the cliff into the sea.'

'What?'

'Oh yes,' said the penguin. 'It's an old family tradition. All us Tristan da Cunha penguins do it.'

'Well, do it now and do it very quickly,' said the Hearse Whisperer. 'Here, I'll help you.'

She kicked the little penguin and it slid down the ice faster than a sliding penguin.

'Thank y o o o o o o u u u u . . .' it shouted as it shot off the cliff top, across over the grass and rocks, past a small fishing boat, right over the heads of seven very impressed seals, and landed in the sea over eighty metres from the shore. Even the

Hearse Whisperer had to admit, though only to herself, that the penguin's slide had looked pretty impressive.

The tiny bird ploughed through the waves, disappeared into the surf and bobbed up waving its little wings at all the other penguins, who gave it a high-five and cheered as only small penguins bobbing about in frantic surf can.

The Hearse Whisperer's veins were at bursting point. How could she have been so stupid? How could she have let those vile Floods trick her again? She stared down into the volcano and concentrated. The bottom of the crater was shaped like a heart, which made her even more angry.[24] A tiny crack appeared in the ice. The volcano's last eruption had been in 1961. That had only been a baby, even though it had meant everyone had had to leave the island for a couple of years.

'This one will wipe the island off the face of the earth,' she sneered. 'Unless. Hold on . . .'

Maybe the Floods had been double bluffing. Maybe they had suspected she would think that Tristan da Cunha was a false trail. So maybe they really were on their way there after all, thinking that she would think they weren't and be a long way away.

Fuzzy black spots appeared in front of her eyes. Her veins stopped getting ready to burst and

---

24 *This is absolutely true. Look at it here: http://www.tristandc.com/peak.php*

started throbbing. Just how many she knew, they knew she knew, she knew they knew she knews could there be?

'Why does life have to be so complicated?' she cried.

'Because if it wasn't, you would be out of work,' she answered herself. 'And life would be boring.'

'Right now,' she continued, 'I wouldn't mind a bit of boring.'

She was now seriously depressed because she knew that having conversations with yourself was only one short step away from sitting in a chair smelling of wee and having conversations with the wall like her old grandmother used to do. Depressed was the normal mood for the Hearse Whisperer. She felt happy and safe that way, but this was way below that kind of depression. And there wasn't even a wall to hit her head against.

Let's face it, she thought, *I have become an emo.*

And it was all the Floods' fault.

The cold was getting to her. She began to fantasise about leaving planet Earth, about transporting herself up to the international space station and then blasting the whole of planet Earth into oblivion. That would finish the Floods off wherever they were hiding.

Trouble is, she thought, *it would finish off all my friends and family too.*

She thought for a bit longer, then concluded, *But I haven't got any friends and I hate my family, so maybe it's worth looking into.*

'I'm getting too old for this job,' she said out loud and then set about destroying every single living thing – fourteen slugs, eighty-three ants and a lost snail – that might have heard her say it.

CHAPTER 11

The door had slowly creaked open a crack, but the Floods still couldn't see who was inside.

'Go away,' said a voice.

'We were wondering if you could put us up for the night,' said Mordonna.

'We're closed,' said the voice. 'For renovations.'

'And we've come for the dog,' said Mildred. 'My dog.'

'I said . . .' the voice began and then stopped.

The door opened wide to reveal a thin, ashen-faced man who bore a strange resemblance to Valla

– which is to say, he bore a strange resemblance to a long-dead corpse.

'Dog?' said the man.

'Yes, her dog,' said Mordonna.

'Oh my Lord,' said the man. 'You are Mildred Flambard, the last witch to die here under the merciful hands of the Knights Intolerant. How can this be?'

'As you can see,' said Mildred, 'I am no longer dead.'

'I, I, I . . .' said the man.

'You, you, you,' said Mildred. 'You are Standpipe the butler and you took as much delight in my suffering as I shall in yours.'

'No, please,' said Standpipe. 'Hear my words, words I dared not speak those many years ago.'

'Go on.'

'I do not believe there is such a thing as witches, nor did I then,' said Standpipe. 'But to have said as much to the Knights Intolerant would have been to sign my own death warrant.'

'So why were you so cruel?' said Mildred.

'Erm, no, listen,' Standpipe begged, 'I am a nice person. I am kind to animals. Have I not kept your dog alive these past two hundred years?'

'I don't know, have you? We haven't seen him.'

'Can you not hear him howl?'

'That could be a recording,' said Winchflat.

'Recorders weren't invented two hundred years ago,' said Standpipe.

'Well, maybe the dog died only a few years ago,' said Betty. 'And happy dogs don't howl. Only sad ones do that.'

'Or else you invented the very first sound recorder a long time before anyone else,' said Merlinmary.

'Or you have invented a brilliant time machine sound recorder that can capture noises from times gone by,' said Winchflat.

'Or the dog is still alive,' Standpipe whimpered.

He seemed to shrink to half his size, a small pathetic creature with a runny nose and mould in

his hair. He moved his head slowly from side to side, staring open-mouthed at the Floods.

'Oh my Lord,' he cried. 'I was wrong. There are real witches and wizards and Mildred Flambard was not the last of them and you are all wizards and I –'

'Yes,' said Mordonna. 'Now go and fetch the dog before I turn you into a toad.'

'I can't,' said Standpipe.

'Why not?'

'It hates me. Although I have fed and watered it for the past two hundred years, it hates me with all its heart and if I ever go too near, it tries to tear me apart.'

'All the more reason to send you to fetch it,' said Mildred.

'I'll fetch it,' said Winchflat.

'It might be a trap,' said Mordonna.

'It'll be OK,' said Winchflat. 'Besides, there's something down there that I need to check on.'

'What?'

'You'll see.'

He left the room and went down to the cellars. Almost immediately, the mournful howling stopped and was replaced by happy yelps.

'He never did that for me,' said Standpipe. 'Not once in two hundred years.'

'Well, look at you,' said Mordonna. 'You're a disgrace to whatever species it is you belong to. Who on earth would be happy to see you?'

'I expect his mother was,' said Betty, who was the kindest one of the Floods.

'She wasn't, actually,' said Standpipe. 'She put me out with the garbage when I was three. I sat by the kerb in the garbage bin for a week because the garbage men refused to take me. When they came back a week later she gave them ten dollars and then they took me.'

'That's terrible,' said Betty.

'Did they give her any change?' sniggered Merlinmary.

'Yes, nine dollars,' said Standpipe. 'How did you know?'

'What did they do with you?' said Betty.

'Two streets away they threw me off the back of the cart into the mud.'

'But surely you could have just gone back home, couldn't you?' said Betty.

'Oh yes,' said Standpipe. 'I did, but in the hour since I had left, my parents had sold the house and moved and refused to tell anyone where they were going.'

'You poor man,' said Betty. 'So you never saw your parents again?'

'Only bits of them,' said Standpipe. 'When the Knights Intolerant took me in and I told them my sad tale, they tracked my parents down.'

'So you were reunited after all?' said Betty.

'Partly,' said Standpipe. 'The Knights chopped them into little bits. All I saw of my parents were their left ears. They were so good to me, the

Knights Intolerant, they had those ears made into a beautiful purse. Look, I have it here still with the three coppers the knights gave me for my twenty years of loyal service.'

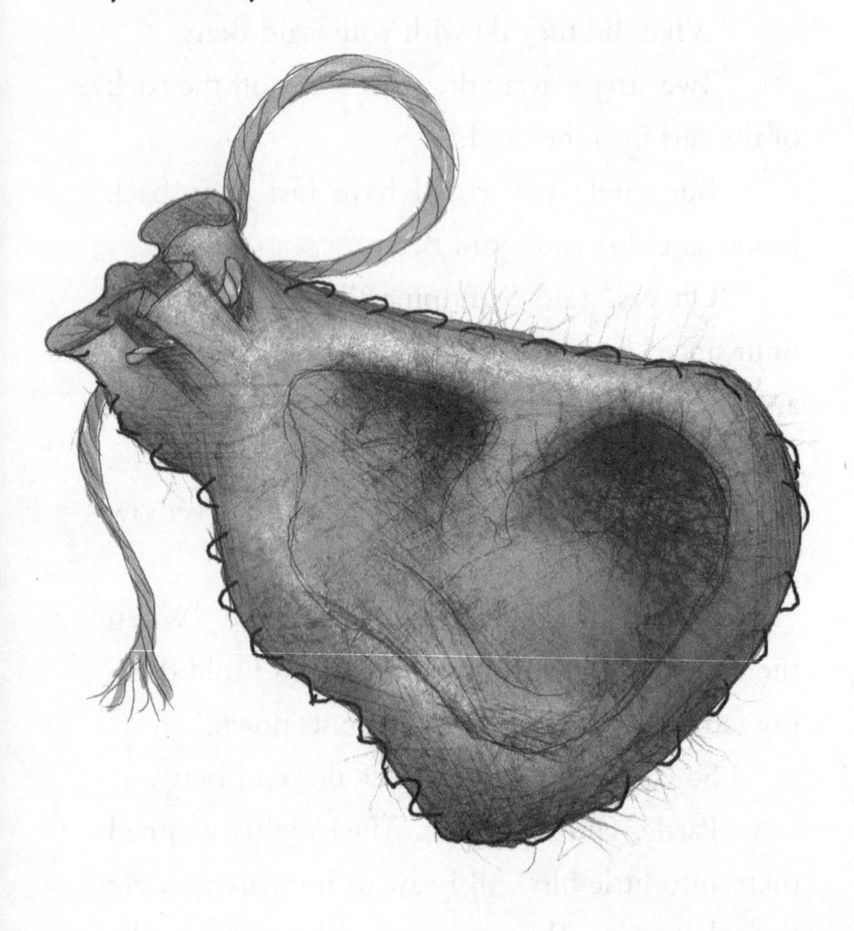

'Oh, you poor, poor man,' said Betty.

'No he's not,' said Mildred. 'He's pure evil. Look.'

She pulled her left sleeve up and burnt into her skin was a scar. It read:

PAINMAKER STANDPIPE
BESPOKE TORTURING
TO THE ARISTOCRACY
SERIOUS AGONY AND SCARRING
OR YOUR MONEY BACK

'Oh,' said Betty. 'Fair enough. Let's take him down to the cellars and chain him up where your poor dog was.'

'Winchflat's taking his time,' said Mordonna, 'and it's gone very quiet.'

She went over to Standpipe and, clicking her fingers, made him rise up into the air. There was a large iron chandelier hanging from the ceiling and Standpipe floated over to it. The chandelier had once held fifty-one candles, one for each of the

Knights Intolerant. Standpipe reached out and grabbed it, clambering up into the middle of the ornate steelwork. Mordonna clicked her fingers again and fifty-one large yellow candles filled the chandelier, fifty-one candles with big yellow flames that imprisoned Standpipe in a circle of fire.

'Tell me,' Mordonna said. 'The Knights Intolerant, are any of them still alive?'

'They are, all fifty-one of them, but they are old and toothless and all near extinction,' Standpipe cried. 'They all lie in their beds in the Great Dormitory awaiting death.'

'Really. And their weapons?'

'They lie rusted away in the Great Sword Room.'

'So they are powerless?'

'Yes,' said Standpipe. 'They are like me, old and feeble, living out our last days on nettle soup and weevil biscuits.'

'But in their time they killed many, many witches and wizards,' said Queen Scratchrot. 'They

almost drove our race to extinction, and being old and feeble is no release from being guilty.'

'I, I, I . . .' Standpipe whispered. 'I cannot disagree.'

The heat from the fifty-one candles was ferocious, as had been the wrath of the fifty-one Knights Intolerant. Standpipe poured with sweat as he clung to the chain. Mordonna handed him a steel rod with a little cup on the end.

'Take this,' she said, 'and snuff out the candles. As each one dies so will each one of the evil Knights Intolerant.'

'I cannot,' whimpered Standpipe.

'Of course you can,' said Mordonna. 'Don't be such a baby. It's your one chance to redeem yourself and possibly save your own neck.'

'Oh, all right,' said Standpipe and began snuffing out the candles.

As each candle died and Standpipe moved the steel cup on to the next one, the dead candle sprang back to life.

'Betty, stop doing that,' said Mordonna.

'Sorry, Mum, I couldn't resist,' said Betty.

'I know, sweetheart, but this is a seriously gothic moment of great symbolism. So stop it,' said Mordonna. 'When all of the candles are gone, witches and wizards around the world will be free.'

'We're free already,' said Valla. 'I mean, most of us hadn't even heard of these crazy knights.'

'I know, darling,' Mordonna replied. 'It's symbolic more than real, though I'm sure that hidden deep inside the soul of every wizard is an ancient memory of persecution by the knights, a memory that we are about to finish off forever.'

'OK,' said Betty. 'Sorry, Mum.'

One by one Standpipe put out the candles until there was only one left.

'This is a truly great moment,' said Queen Scratchrot, peering out from her backpack with her one good eye.

But the last candle wouldn't die.

'Betty!'

'It's not me, Mum. I'm not doing anything.'

Mildred Flambard-Flood fell to her knees and

wept. She buried her head in her hands and shed floods of tears onto the ancient flagstones.

'It is me,' she cried. 'That last candle is my father.'

'Your own father was one of the Knights Intolerant?' said Mordonna.

'Yes.'

'And you cannot bear to see him die?'

'You must be joking,' said Mildred. 'After what he did to mother and I? No, these are tears of relief and joy. I feel as if I have been holding my breath these past two hundred years. Actually, I was holding my breath until my precious Valla rescued me. So let me be the one to kill the flame.'

So she sat on Valla's shoulders, who stood on Nerlin's shoulders, and she grabbed the steel cup from Standpipe and slammed it down on the last candle.

'And as for you,' she said, turning to Standpipe, 'did you really think snuffing out a few candles would make up for all the terrible things you did to me and my mother and countless other witches?'

'But . . .' Standpipe began, turning to Mordonna. 'You promised.'

'No, she said "possibly save your life", not definitely,' said Mildred. 'Do we look like Love and Peace Greenie Buddhists? Do we look like hippies? Don't answer that bit.'

She clicked her fingers and Standpipe vanished in a pile of dust.

'Wow,' she said. 'I haven't done magic for two hundred years. I'd forgotten just how good it feels.'

She clicked her fingers and three cockroaches that had been sitting on the chandelier next to Standpipe turned into a box of paperclips, a bowl of muesli and a copy of the first ever *Batman* comic.

At the same moment, Winchflat and Brastof came up from the cellar. The dog raced over to Mildred and leapt up into her arms, licking her face and madly wagging his tail – which, considering Mildred was still sitting on Valla's shoulders, who was still standing on Nerlin's shoulders, shows not only how much Brastof had missed her, but also how incredibly high he could jump.

'That is Brastof?' said Mordonna. 'I kind of pictured him as a huge black hound, not a spaniel.'

'He certainly barks like a big black hound,' said Nerlin.

'Oh, I did that,' said Mildred. 'He had such a girly little yap that even mice laughed at him.'

'Until I speaked,' Brastof said. 'They usually went srsly quiet then.'

'So tell me,' said Mordonna, 'could you speak when you were born, or did your wonderful mistress teach you?'

'Mistrss dun magik,' said Brastof. 'Not too good wiv speling tho. Srsly.'

Mordonna gave Mildred a hug and a huge smile.

'You were so made to be part of our family,' she said.

'And so were you,' said Satanella to Brastof.

There were so many ways that Brastof was meant to be part of the ever-growing Floods family. They included, in no special order of importance:

- *Satanella needed a boyfriend.*
- *He could talk.*
- *He had his own red rubber ball – although, as it was over two hundred years old, it had lost a lot of its bounce.*
- *His smell was exactly the same as Queen Scratchrot's armpits.*

- *He was very cheap to look after – after all, he had survived for two centuries on three tins of Pedigree Chum, seventeen spiders, lots of rats' legs and a brussels sprout.*
- *He knew of lot of really rude jokes.*

There is, hidden away in a remote valley[25] in Transylvania Waters, a special clinic. Only 0.5 per cent of the population know this valley exists. It isn't on any maps, on account of none of Transylvania Waters being on any maps, but even if there was a map of Transylvania Waters, this valley would NOT be on it because it's a secret. Of the 0.5 per

[25] *I know, as you should by now, that every single part of Transylvania Waters is remote, but this valley is the most remote bit of the whole country. Very few people who actually live in Transylvania Waters have heard of it and even one really stupid goatherd who lives in the actual valley hasn't heard of it.*

cent who know it exists, only thirty-seven of them know there is a clinic there and only half of those thirty-seven know what the clinic is for – and seven of the ones who know what it's for work there.[26]

To summarise, this clinic is more remote, more exclusive and more secretive than anywhere else on Earth, even that place in the Nevada desert where the American government keeps some dead aliens from outer space.

One of the thirty-seven people who knew about the clinic was the Hearse Whisperer.

And she has just gone there.

This is the Sulfuric Clinic, a special hospital for the treatment of depression and insanity in witches and wizards. Its director and owner is the fearsome Dr Reversion.

Dr Reversion was a powerful woman. She had more muscles than most men, even serious body builders, and other muscles that most men would never want if, that is, they even knew such

[26] *Yes, I know half of thirty-seven is eighteen and a half, but if you ever meet the strange half person, you'll understand.*

muscles existed. Tall, with damp black shiny hair, Dr Reversion wore a lot of damp black shiny leather that cried in pain as she moved, because some of the leather belonged to animals that were still alive. Notebook and pen in one hand, damp black shiny whip in the other, Dr Reversion was the perfect psychiatrist for a depressed wizard. For depressed witches, maybe not so perfect, but as she was actually a witch herself and the only psychiatrist specialising in the treatment of screwed-up wizards and witches, she was as perfect as they were going to get.

'I cannot believe it,' she said. 'The legendary Hearse Whisperer here in my clinic.'

The Hearse Whisperer had left a webcam on the volcano rim on Tristan da Cunha, a webcam that sent its pictures right into her brain so she would know the instant the Floods arrived – if they arrived. Then she had transformed and flown back to Transylvania Waters.

To get into the clinic as a patient and not as dinner – albatross stew was one of Dr Reversion's favourite meals – she had had to transform herself

again, but she felt her miserable state of mind was worth it. It had snowed a lot more on Tristan since she had left, and now the camera was buried in a deep drift. All the Hearse Whisperer could see inside her head was pure white, the colour she hated more than any other colour in the whole world. This, of course, was making her even more depressed.

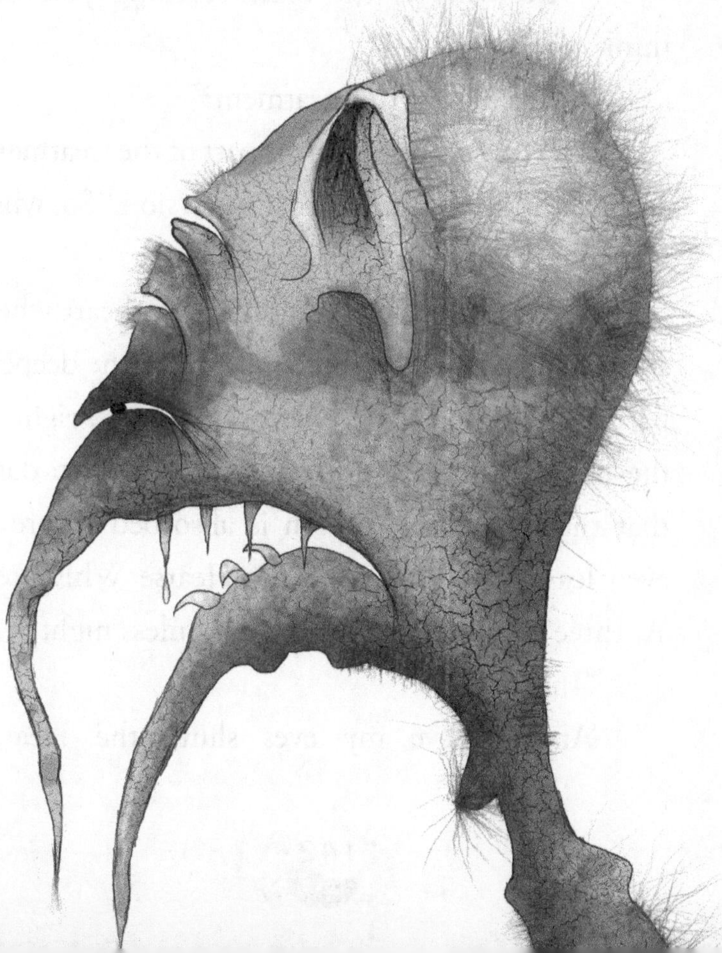

'When I was a child,' said Dr Reversion, 'I had your picture on my bedroom wall. Well, I say your picture, but as you know, there are no pictures of you, so I had a huge sheet of black paper taped up right above my head.'

'How black was it?' said the Hearse Whisperer, fearing grey.

'Well, what is the blackest thing you can think of?'

'Is this part of the treatment?'

'Of course. Everything is part of the treatment at the Sulfuric Clinic,' said Dr Reversion. 'So, what is the blackest thing you can think of?'

'The centre of my grandmother's heart when she was sitting in a locked cupboard in the deepest part of the Transylvania Waters coal mine, right at the bottom of shaft thirteen, where it is so dark that the light from a torch is absorbed before it even leaves the bulb,' said the Hearse Whisperer. 'At three a.m. on a completely moonless night.'

'That is good.'

'And I have my eyes shut,' the Hearse

Whisperer added. 'And I am wearing a blindfold made of lead lined with black velvet.'

'Excellent,' said Dr Reversion, 'an answer worthy of the legendary Hearse Whisperer. Now I can tell you that the huge black poster on my wall that represented you was ten times darker than that.'

'Ten times darker?' the Hearse Whisperer said. 'Is that possible?'

'Oh yes,' said Dr Reversion. 'Do not forget you are the Hearse Whisperer. You are a legend and as such you deserve the blackest black in creation, a black that is not merely the absence of all colour, but the absence of black itself.'

'You're not just saying that to make me feel better?' said the Hearse Whisperer.

'Well, of course I am,' said Dr Reversion, but before her patient could look upset, she added, 'and you *should* feel better, because it is true.'

'Already, I feel a great weight beginning to lift from my shoulders,' said the Hearse Whisperer.

She felt her spirits rise. The last time she had

felt her spirits rise, she had let them rise just above her shoulders and then she had torn their heads off and eaten them raw with a green salad. Her spirits had kept their heads down since then, but now they were rising again. This time, however, the doctor told her to let them fly free.

'See them hovering below the ceiling?' said the doctor. 'If you don't mind me saying so, some of them are rather overweight. So it's not surprising you feel the weight lifting. We will deal with them in a moment – but first, tell me why you are here. I mean, what on earth could make you, one of the most powerful and evil witches in the world, so depressed?'

'The Floods.'

'Ahh, I see,' said the doctor. 'You feel the Floods are your nemesis?'

'Oh no, that was my grandmother.'

'Your grandmother was your nemesis?'

'No, no, she was my only comforter,' said the Hearse Whisperer. 'Nemesis was her name.'

'So what do the Floods represent?'

'Failure,' said the Hearse Whisperer, dropping her head as her spirits began to fall again.

Dr Reversion handed her an umbrella.

'Here,' she said, 'take this. It will keep your spirits off.'

The Hearse Whisperer said nothing. Her spirits were rising and falling like yoyos. One minute they were soaring and hitting their heads on the ceiling. The next they were bouncing off her umbrella and grovelling on the floor. Dr Reversion suggested that they go outside. The next time the Hearse Whisperer's spirits soared, they vanished up into the clouds. The Hearse Whisperer and Dr Reversion ran back inside and locked the door.

'And now,' the doctor said, 'when we have stabilised you and you are totally dispirited, or, as I prefer to say, Spirit Cleansed, we can take you into the Transferation Laboratory and give you a spirit transplant.'

'What?'

'We can give you a spirit transplant,' said the doctor. 'We have a huge store of brand new and

second-hand spirits, from Happy Fluffy Bunny to Leap Into Prams And Eat The Baby. I don't see you as a Happy Fluffy Bunny and we've had problems with the Baby Eater. No matter how many times we de-bug them we can never completely remove the trace of guilt or the indigestion.'

'Well, right now, I'd like the Curled Up Asleep In Bed,' said the Hearse Whisperer, 'with added Never Wake Up Again.'

'Oh dear, oh dear,' said Dr Reversion. 'I didn't realise you were in such a bad way. I think we will have to give you acupuncture.'

'Whatever,' said the Hearse Whisperer.

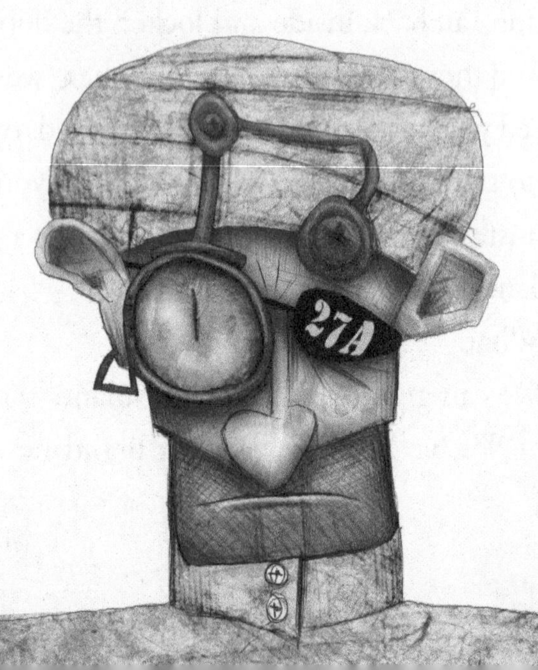

'Sit,' the doctor commanded and, as she left the room, she added, 'Stay.'

Choose from the following reasons why she left the room. You may choose more than one answer:

- *She was going to get the acupuncture hammer and nails.*
- *She was bored.*
- *It was lunchtime.*
- *She needed to go to the toilet.*
- *She was actually a robot and her batteries were going flat.*
- The Bold & The Beautiful *was about to start on TV.*
- *She was overcome with even more depression than the Hearse Whisperer, having just discovered her heroine was not invincible but old and tired and depressed.*
- *She had heard the ice-cream van outside and was dying for a Cornetto.*

- *Some of the above.*
- *All of the above.*
- *None of the above.*
- *None of the below.*
- *Dog food.*
- *Toilet rolls.*
- *Vinegar.*[27]

The Hearse Whisperer lay back on the examination couch and closed her eyes. Everything was still white and a thousand thoughts, some evil, some miserable, some seriously weird, all fought for her attention. These included imagining the long list of things the King would do to her if she failed to bring his precious Mordonna home to him. The traditional water-skiing on Lake Tarnish, an honour the King reserved for his enemies, would be mild compared to what the King would do to her. Thoughts of moving to a foreign country

[27] *Oops, seem to have got muddled up with my shopping list.*

under a false name came into her head, but where could she go?

She had no friends and the few relations she had who were still alive – or at least sane enough to not spend all day talking to a stain on the wall – were all in Transylvania Waters, and that was probably the last place she should go. Of course, she was there already, but pretended she wasn't because visiting the Sulfuric Clinic was something you kept very quiet about. In fact, the clinic provided its patients with a special service where they sent postcards to your friends and family pretending you were having a wonderful holiday in Bali. All this was irrelevant because the Hearse Whisperer had stopped talking to her relatives three weeks before she had been born, apart from her beloved grandmother, who was deaf anyway so it didn't really matter.

And then two and two added together and were joined by six and a half and the Hearse Whisperer thought, *If Transylvania Waters is the last place I should go, then my enemies would think*

that too, so in actual fact, as long as I stayed indoors, Transylvania Waters is probably the safest place I could go because it would be the last place anyone would expect me to be.

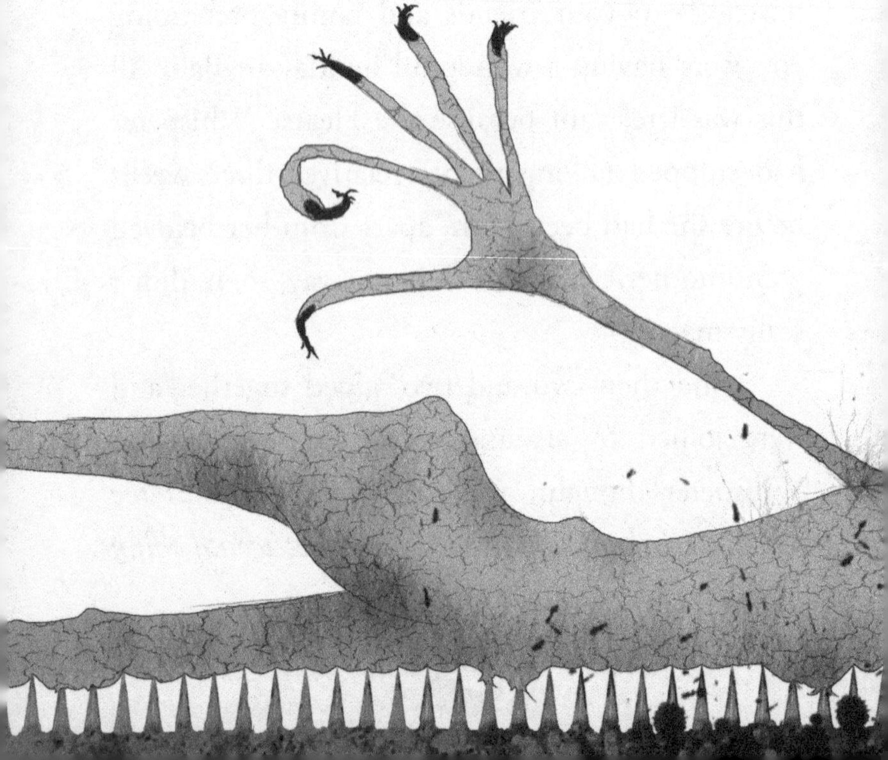

And then, just as an even more totally brilliant thought was about to replace that one, something else hit her, but it wasn't the brilliant thought. It was Dr Reversion's first acupuncture nail and that knocked all thoughts and ideas out of her head with the most painful agony she had ever felt.[28]

'AAAHHHHHHHHH!' the Hearse Whisperer screamed as the first nail was knocked into her left ear.

'F@@#XXX!!!!£,' she cried as another nail went in through her right ear.

'GR!!***&∞¢¢KK*!' as another went up her nose.

---

[28] *And painful agony was one of the Hearse Whisperer's favourite things, something she had enjoyed many, many times and considered herself to be something of a connoisseur of.*

'This might hurt a little bit,' said Dr Reversion, holding up a really big nail.

'Might? Might?' cried the Hearse Whisperer. 'Why didn't you warn me before?'

'I wanted you to be nice and relaxed,' said the doctor, knocking in a few more nails.

'Relaxed,' the Hearse Whisperer whimpered. 'I haven't been relaxed since 1965.'

'Well, try to relax now while the nails go to work,' said the doctor. 'Here, have a toffee. I'll be back in an hour.'

Mackerel, Mackerel, Mackerel, F@@#XXX!!!!£!!, Organiser!!!, thought the Hearse Whisperer as she fought to stay conscious through the excruciating pain.

But gradually the pain subsided, partly due to the incredibly powerful sedatives in the toffee and partly because the agony was making her faint. Floaty hippy music tinkled from hidden speakers and the Hearse Whisperer felt herself drifting back in time.

The sky turned a beautiful green colour like

the skies of her childhood when all that lovely acid rain had drifted over Transylvania Waters, making everyone wonderfully white as it bleached their skin. The Hearse Whisperer was a little girl again, playing in the back garden of the childhood home she had only had inside her head. There were the kittens she had nailed to the fence. There were the blindfolded chickens walking into the bonfire. And there was her beloved grandmother, collecting the pretty berries from the belladonna plants to make her delicious purple custard.

But where was her Mama?

'Mama, mama,' she cried.

'Yes,' said a voice. 'Where are your parents?'

'I, I . . .'

'You had them locked up in prison on Howlcatraz, didn't you?' said the voice. It was Dr Reversion.

That broke the spell.

'No I didn't,' said the Hearse Whisperer, sitting bolt upright.

This was a bad move as she still had the

acupuncture nails sticking into her. She screamed and fell backwards as, one by one, the doctor removed them. Now her only problem was blood spouting from all the nail holes.

'That's it, let it all out,' said the doctor. 'Let it go.'

'What, all my blood?'

'Yes, every evil drop, as you did to your mother and father.'

'I didn't lock up my parents,' said the Hearse Whisperer. 'They were carried away by vampires.'

'But it says in your notes that you locked up your mother and your father for being too nice. It also says that this is something you used to be very proud of. Yet now you are denying it as if you feel shame for what you did,' said Dr Reversion.

'No, no, that's not true,' said the Hearse Whisperer. 'I have never felt shame.'

'Are you absolutely sure?'

'I think I'd remember if I'd done something as pathetic as that,' the Hearse Whisperer replied. 'Look at me, I am a totally shame-free zone.'

'Well, no, not necessarily, you see, because the mind has a way of suppressing things that we might be ashamed of,' said the doctor.

'Yes, but if I had got my parents sent to prison, why would I deny that? I mean, it's not like it's a bad thing to do, is it?' said the Hearse Whisperer. 'People do it all the time, don't they?'

'That's true, but there's something else, isn't there?' said the doctor.

'No.'

'Come on. It was in the papers. You were voted Creation's Most Evil Being because of it.'

'Oh, that,' said the Hearse Whisperer, torn between pride and denial.

'Yes, that,' said the doctor. 'You appeared to have had a total change of heart and got your parents set free and everyone thought you had gone soft, but then it turned out you'd had them released so you could eat them. Remember?'

'Well, they deserved it. Everyone said so, even Grandmother and all my other relations. In fact, I – I mean we – had a big party afterwards and

they all helped eat them,' the Hearse Whisperer explained.

'I thought you said you had stopped speaking to your family,' said the doctor.

'Yes, I did.'

'But now you're saying you had a big party.'

'We did, but I also said we were eating my parents,' said the Hearse Whisperer. 'And as everyone knows, it's very bad manners to talk with your mouth full.'

'Do you want to talk about it?' said the doctor, who was a bit of a cannibalism enthusiast.

'Not particularly.'

'Are you sure?'

'Yes, I'm sure.'

'Oh, OK.'

'So could you stop me bleeding now?' said the Hearse Whisperer. 'I'm feeling rather faint. In fact, I think I'm approaching a Becoming-Dead situation.'

'Do you want to talk about that?'

'No, I just want it to stop.'

'Do you want to talk about why you want it to stop?'

'No, I, er . . .'

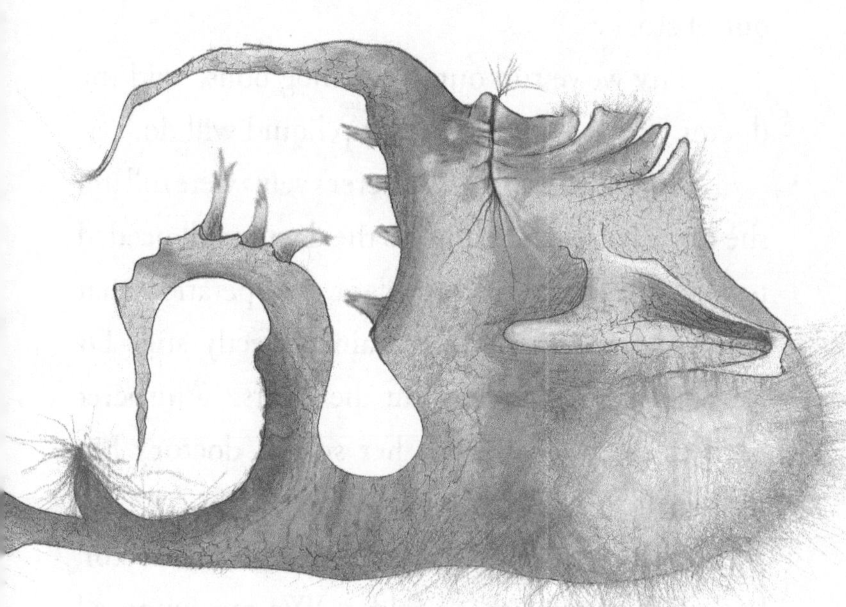

Dr Reversion felt the Hearse Whisperer's pulse and, when it had finally stopped beating, one of her assistants wheeled the body into the Transferation Laboratory. They laid her out on a black marble slab, stuck corks in all the holes left

by the acupuncture nails and began to fill her up with fresh blood, a special recipe tailored exactly to suit her particular needs, or rather Dr Reversion's needs, give or take a few species that were currently out of stock.[29]

'Pity we've run out of warthog boils,' said the doctor, 'but I think washing-up liquid will do.'

Once the Hearse Whisperer's veins were full up, she came back to life, but, as the doctor still needed to perform the spirit transplant, an operation that required the patient to remain perfectly still, Dr Reversion was forced to put the Hearse Whisperer back to sleep again with her special doctor's Big Rubber Hammer.

'Spirits, spirits . . . let me see,' said the doctor, leafing through a thick folder. 'We are supposed to give her back her terrifying motivation and her evil, reckless edge and love of mindless violence. I imagine that's what she wants.'

'Of course, Doctor,' said her laboratory

---

[29] *For the exact recipe of the blood that Dr Reversion poured into the Hearse Whisperer's veins, see the back of this book.*

assistant, Flusher, 'but do you not think that maybe she is actually too old to contain all that fury?'

'Yes, you're quite right,' said Dr Reversion. 'Sad, isn't it? And anyway, I have no intention of restoring her to her former glory. You see, when I was growing up, the Hearse Whisperer was my greatest hero – a magnificent, totally invincible creature who I worshipped. But I wrote to her seventy-three times and do you know how many times she replied?'

'No.'

'None,' said the doctor.

'So you feel cheated and disillusioned?'

'Of course I do,' said the doctor.

'Do you want to talk about it?' said Flusher.

'Careful now, that's my line.'

'Sorry,' said Flusher. 'Well, would you like to have some revenge?'

'I would, I would.'

'Well, now *you* are the one with the power,' said Flusher.

'I am, aren't I?' The doctor laughed and,

flicking through her spirit catalogue, she added, 'It's payback time.'

She gave the Hearse Whisperer another highly skilled and professional whack on the head with the Big Rubber Hammer and drilled a hole in the top of her skull.

'Right, where shall we start?' she said, poking a funnel into the hole.

She closed the catalogue, shut her eyes and picked a page at random.

Obsessed With Flower Arranging

'Brilliant!' said Flusher, as she uncorked the bottle. 'Do another one.'

Forgetting Everything You Ever Learned About Potty Training

Flusher and the doctor collapsed on the floor laughing. They tried to pull themselves up but

each time they reached table height, one look at the Hearse Whisperer lying unconscious on the operating table made them collapse again.

Sewage Taster

'Not sure about that one, she might enjoy it.'

'You know what, doctor?' said Flusher in a voice of deep admiration. 'I think you were wasting yourself adoring the Hearse Whisperer. You are every bit as evil as she is.'

'Do you really think so?'

'You also have wonderful knees,' said Flusher.

They gave the Hearse Whisperer another seven feeble unpleasant souls, three of which hated the other four, which meant she had a permanent headache. Then, while she was still unconscious, they sent her back to the volcano's rim on Tristan da Cunha.

'Shouldn't we give her a blanket?' said Flusher. 'There's a blizzard blowing.'

'Then she'll have a nice blanket of thick snow,' said Dr Reversion.

'But she could freeze to death.'

'Promises, promises.'

'What was it you wanted to look at in the cellar?' Betty asked Winchflat. 'When you went to get Brastof you said there was something down there you wanted to check up on.'

'Yes, little sister, well remembered,' said Winchflat.

'So what was it?'

'You know I said there were six Terrible Pools of Vestor?' said Winchflat.

'Yes.'

'Well, five of them are a chain of Yak Burger restaurants in Mongolia and the sixth one, the

real Terrible Pool of Vestor, is right here under this very building in a dark catacomb next to the dungeons.'

'F@@#XXX!!!!£,' screeched Vessel with excitement. 'Who's a pretty boy? Who's a pretty boy? Who's a pretty boy?'

'You are, my darling,' said the Queen. 'What are we waiting for?'

'As well as the good news, which is that I've found the Terrible Pool of Vestor,' said Winchflat, 'there is bad news, which is that it's sort of evaporated.'

'You mean it's all gone?' said the Queen.

Winchflat nodded.

'So you haven't so much found the Terrible Pool of Vestor as the Dent In The Ground That Used To Be The Terrible Pool Of Vestor?' said Mordonna.

'Exactly.'

'If it's not there any more,' said Nerlin, 'how do you know it is the Terrible Pool?'

'There's a brass plate saying, "In this dent lay

the Terrible Pool of Vestor",' said Winchflat.

'Double, triple GR!!***&∞¢¢KK*!' said Vessel.

'You can say that again,' said the Queen, so he did. 'Is there nothing we can do?'

'There is a little bit of dust left in the bottom,' said Winchflat. 'Maybe we could add water to it and bring the pool back to life.'

'OK, let's go,' said Nerlin. 'Someone get a bucket.'

'I should warn you,' said Winchflat. 'There's a strong possibility that the dust is not pure. It could have all sorts of pollution in it. I mean, supposing someone was sweeping the floor? It's the obvious place to dump the dust, isn't it?'

'We'll risk it,' said the Queen. 'Get the bucket.'

'What would happen,' said Mordonna, 'if one of us who hadn't been turned into a bird and trapped in an enchanted cage went into the pool?'

'I don't know,' said Winchflat. 'There's no information on that.'

'Well, before we put Vessel and his cage in the the pool, I suggest we put someone else in and see what happens,' said Valla.

'Who?' said Betty. 'I'm not going to volunteer.'

'None of the children can volunteer,' said the Queen. 'If anyone is going to test out the pool, it should be me.'

'OK,' said Mordonna.

'Aren't you going to protest a little bit?' said the Queen. 'After all, it could be dangerous.'

'No,' said Mordonna. 'You're the obvious choice.'

'Yes, I am, aren't I,' said the Queen through gritted teeth.[30]

'And you can carry the birdcage in with you,' said Mordonna. 'That way whatever happens you will both be together.'

'F@@#XXX!!!!£,' Vessel whispered to himself.

---

[30] *The Queen's teeth had been gritted since she had been dropped on the beach while on holiday recently with her family. See* The Floods 6: The Great Outdoors.

When the pool had been filled to the brim, Winchflat tipped the Queen out of her backpack and did his best to join all her bones and floppy insides back together. One leg seemed to be a lot shorter than the other until he realised he had joined her left arm on where her left leg should be. Two of her fingers were stuck so far up her nose it was impossible to remove them, but eventually Queen Scratchrot stood proudly before them looking as wonderful as only a half-decomposed corpse with green slime leaking from way too many places can look. Because the Queen's remaining fingers refused to talk to each other, Winchflat tied Vessel's cage round her neck and led them to the pool's edge.

'Ready?' he said.

'Umm, er, not really,' said the Queen. 'Maybe we should talk about this a bit more.'

'No time,' said Winchflat. 'Bits of you are falling off as you stand there.'

'Here, take this,' he added, picking up her right ear.

'GR!!***&∞¢¢KK*!' Vessel screeched as the

Queen hesitated at the water's edge.

'Oh get on with it,' snapped Mordonna and gave her mother an almighty shove.

Big splash.

Waves.

Queen and cage vanishing below the water's surface.

Water calming down until it was as smooth as a sheet of glass.

Then nothing.

'Oops,' said Mordonna.

More nothing and, several minutes later, even more nothing.

Then a single bubble.

Then a lot more bubbles accompanied by everyone holding their noses and waving their hands in front of their faces.

'It's supposed to do that,' Winchflat lied. 'I think it's all the bad stuff coming out.'

Actually, he was completely right, except the bad stuff was *really* bad, and boy was there a lot of it.

'Whatever you do,' said Nerlin, trying not to breathe in as he spoke, 'no one light a match.'

Everyone except Mordonna backed away from the pool, ran out of the door, up the stairs and out into the fresh air. Mordonna alone stood vigil as the foul bubbles poured out their grey fumes, but eventually they began to lessen. The grey fumes clung to the sludge-covered wall of the cellar, turning to slime. As they did so, the

air cleared until it was safe to breathe again. The last bubble burst and the pool grew flat and still again.

As Mordonna watched and waited, Betty came back and took hold of her hand.

'Is Granny dead?'

'I'm not sure, darling,' said Mordonna. 'I don't think so. I can feel her presence, but then I can feel the presence of my great-grandmother Florea, and she is most definitely dead.'

The tops of two heads broke the surface of the water. Then two foreheads, four ears and four eyes appeared. More bits of body appeared until Queen Scratchrot and Vessel walked out of the pool and stood before mother and daughter.

'Has it worked?' said the Queen.

Mordonna and Betty were speechless. Not only had the Terrible Pool of Vestor freed Vessel from his cage, it had totally transformed him and the Queen. No longer were they two ancient wrinkled wrecks. The pool had turned back time to the exact day the two of them had left

Transylvania Waters twenty-three years before. They were still quite old, but not so old that bits of them were falling off, and now their wrinkles were not so deep that you could hide things in them.

'You look great,' said Mordonna. 'If I didn't have such perfect skin already, I'd be tempted to take a dip myself.'

But, with the future in mind, she filled a couple of bottles from the pool, and then the four of them went outside to join the others.

'I think we should destroy Forsaken Hall,' said Mildred Flambard-Flood as they got ready to leave. 'We should not just knock it down, but turn it into dust so it can never be used again to bring terror to innocent witches and wizards.'

'You're absolutely right,' said Mordonna. 'We should remove it and, with it, all traces of the Knights Intolerant from the face of the Earth. After all, if someone like the Hearse Whisperer came here, who is to say what she could and would recreate with her evil heart.'

So the family stood side by side and faced the old building and, as they concentrated, it collapsed in on itself. The chimneys fell through the roof. The roof fell through the attic. The attic fell through the upstairs, the upstairs fell through the downstairs and finally the downstairs fell into the cellars.

'Um, what about the Terrible Pool of . . .?' Betty began to say, but it was too late.

The ground shook and heaved and spat and shook again and slowly a totally black tower began to rise from the ground. The walls sucked in all the light around them. Apart from one row of narrow slits just below the overhanging roof, there were no doors or windows in the entire building.

'Oops,' said Mordonna.

'What are we going to do?' said Nerlin.

'We are all going to climb very quietly into the van and drive slowly away,' said Mordonna. 'And then when we get to the next town we are going to go to the planning department of the local council and report an illegally constructed building out on the moors. Then it becomes their problem.'

'Do you really think some small town council officials will be able to tell the Knights Intolerant what to do?' said Valla. 'They'd get obliterated.'

'Well, there you go,' said Mordonna. 'Every cloud has a silver lining.'

What with Mordonna and Nerlin and the seven children and Mildred Flambard-Flood and the Queen and Vessel and Brastof, there was not enough room for everyone inside the old campervan. So as soon as they were out of sight of the tower, Winchflat asked Nerlin to pull over so he could make a few modifications.

He stretched the van a bit, gave it an upstairs level and another four wheels and, while he was at it, improved everything else. No longer would it be confined to roads and tracks. It was now a true All-Terrain Vehicle – not one of those girlie four-

wheel drives that are driven through the dangerous jungles of suburbia where they have to contend with massive obstacles like hamburger containers and puddles, but a true ALL-Terrain Vehicle. Think of any terrain in any dimension and the campervan could traverse it.

'Even the sea?' said Merlinmary.

'Yes, no problem,' said Winchflat, pushing a button.

A big rubber skirt inflated around them as the van turned into a hovercraft.

'Bet it can't fly,' said Morbid.

'Bet it can,' said Winchflat as the doors flew open and began to flap like the wings of a bird.

'Bet it can't . . .' Satanella began.

'Yeah, yeah, yeah,' said Winchflat. 'It can ice-skate, pop a wheelie, break the sound barrier, fly into space and travel in time.'

'Does it have a toilet?' said Betty, as they skimmed over the Mediterranean Sea towards Southern Europe. 'Because I need to go.'

'Umm . . . Hold on a minute.'

'That's the point,' said Betty. 'I can't.'

As soon as they hit land, the van screeched to a halt and Betty ran behind a bush. When she got back Winchflat had added a toilet, a shower, wi-fi internet, a rooftop barbecue and a nodding plastic dog on the dashboard.

'Next time you stop,' said Betty, 'could you find a bush out in the country? The owner of the flower shop was really cross.'

'So are we going to Transylvania Waters now or not?' said Betty.

'Well, yes, if you're all sure,' said Winchflat.

After all his modifications to the VW, he was the only one who knew how to drive it. Nerlin got in a big sulk about this and sat in the back of the van with his back to everybody making engine noises.

'Yes, it's what we all agreed, remember?' said Mordonna.

'I didn't agree,' said Nerlin grumpily. 'I think it's a silly idea.'

Mordonna pointed out that Nerlin had his

doubts about everything, even going to the toilet.

'No I don't,' Nerlin objected.

'You so do, Dad,' said Betty. 'It's always, "Do I need to go or not or should I wait until after lunch?".'

'Doesn't everyone do that?'

'No. Normal people say, " I need to go to the bathroom" and they just go,' said Mordonna.

'Really?' said Nerlin.

'Really.'

'But that takes all the anticipation out of it, all the excitement,' said Nerlin.

'You get excited about going to the toilet?' said Valla.

'Doesn't everyone?'

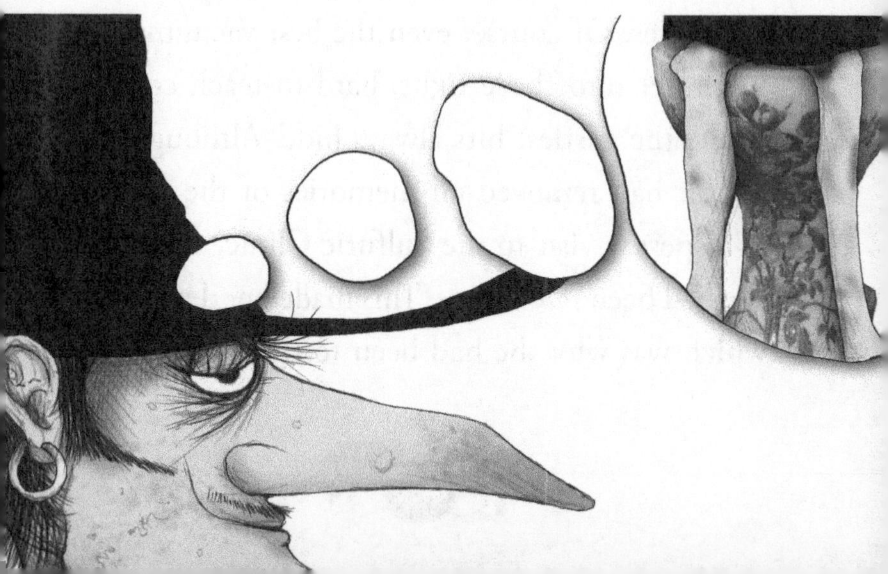

On Tristan da Cunha, the Hearse Whisperer had just regained consciousness. The last thing Dr Reversion had done to her before sending her back there was to poke an Ultrasonic Vacuum Cleaner into her ears and suck out all her recent memories. Of course, even the best vacuums can never get into those tight, hard-to-reach corners where the nastiest bits always hide. Although the doctor had removed all memories of the Hearse Whisperer's visit to the Sulfuric Clinic, she knew she had been *somewhere*. This made her depressed, which was why she had been to the clinic in the

first place. But she comforted herself by thinking that maybe the place she had been to had been a flower shop.

'A flower shop?' she said. 'Don't I hate flowers? All that pretty colour and perfume? Isn't that the opposite of everything I stand for?'

But the Flower Shop Spirit was stuck right in the front of her brain so every time she closed her eyes and tried to visualise something evil like a jagged, rusty, yet really sharp knife, all she could see were yellow chrysanthemums. She concentrated and tried to recall the smell of someone who she had just chopped into little bits, but all she could smell was yellow chrysanthemums.

I feel as if I am only one short step away from sitting in a chair smelling of wee and having conversations with the wall like my old grandmother did, she thought.

'I need help,' she said, but there was no one there to answer her. This was good because she knew that if anyone had heard her say that she would have had to kill them.

Except, she thought, *I wouldn't so much kill them as give them a nice vase of yellow chrysanthemums.*

'I need to go and get help,' she said, but all the information in her head about the Sulfuric Clinic had been vacuumed out and her instinct told her she would get the help she needed in a flower shop.

Then she dug back deep into older memories that the doctor hadn't been able to remove. There was a vague thought that had been nagging the back of her brain. It had been a sudden brilliant thought on the verge of exploding into her consciousness when . . .

What?

There had been a penguin and it had asked her what she was doing, buried up to her neck in snow in the remotest place on Earth, and she had said she was waiting for someone and the penguin had said something . . .

What was it?

'Do you not think that maybe – and this is just an idea – do you not think that this is probably the very last place you would ever meet them?'

YES! That was it!

And then a really, really large penny had dropped, and she had been distracted, but now she was focused.

And she put two and two together with the really, really large penny and the thought jumped up and hit her so hard it gave her a headache.

And the thought was this:

Maybe Tristan da Cunha was not the last place on Earth you would ever meet someone you were looking for. If the someone was the Flood family, maybe the whole remote island thing was a red herring and I hate fish. Maybe there was actually somewhere that was even less likely. Somewhere that was the very, very last place anyone would expect the Floods to go.

Transylvania Waters.

The idea was so unlikely that it was obvious. Or was it all a super, triple, quintuple, double, double bluff, and those bumps in the snow, halfway down the path to Potato Patches, were not just snowdrifts but the Floods. Or not.

The Hearse Whisperer stared at the bumps and concentrated. The snow melted and nine sheep stood there in a confused group with clouds of steam coming off their wool.

'That's it,' said the Hearse Whisperer. 'Time to go home.'

Because sick, evil, double-agent spies get homesick from time to time, so even if the Floods weren't going to Transylvania Waters, it wouldn't be an entirely wasted journey.

Except she thought that she was probably, almost, nearly up to using up her last transformation.

'But when the wretched Floods do come back to Transylvania Waters, I will be waiting,' she laughed, 'and I will teach them a lesson they will never forget. I will teach them flower arranging.'

'No, no, what?' she said. 'It's supposed to be painful and make them dead, those were my orders.'

But the spirits that Dr Reversion had implanted had taken control and as much as she tried, the Hearse Whisperer could not get flower arranging out of her mind.

'There will be gladioli and tulips, and . . . no, no, no,' she cried. 'I need pain and suffering, not floral decorations. I need help. I need to go to . . . um. I need to go to, er, Flowers 'R' Us?'

She screamed and banged her head against the side of the volcano and realised that somehow, somewhere, she had forgotten everything she had ever been taught about potty training and her undies

were full of very, very cold wet yellow patches that were turning to ice.

'Right,' she snapped as she changed into an eagle. 'I am going to Transylvania Waters and I am going to make the Floods arrange flowers until their fingers bleed and there will be poisonous flowers and flowers with sharp thorns. Well, I say poisonous and sharp thorns, but of course the two will have to complement each other so I might have to choose between poisonous or prickly, but there will definitely be one of them. And I'm going to change my undies.'

She threw herself off the edge of the volcano. 'And ferns!' she shouted. 'And mushrooms!'

But as she hadn't actually finished changing into an eagle, she landed on her head on a pointy rock.[31] This was because when a witch gets to the

---

31 *The Hearse Whisperer had been right in thinking that she had almost no transformations left. Dr Reversion had known this and that was the reason she had sent her back to Tristan da Cunha in her real form. She would have to change to leave there and that would weaken her even more.*

last couple of transformations, they can take quite a long time to happen. This time there was a period of at least ten minutes when the Hearse Whisperer had her real body from the knees upwards and an eagle's feet from her knees down.

While she recovered, she pondered the idea of using mushrooms in flower arranging. It appealed to her. It could possibly be a world first. There were some very pretty toadstools and some of them were wonderfully poisonous.

It took the Hearse Whisperer a long time to get back to Transylvania Waters. Not just because she was old and tired, but every time she flew over land, she was distracted by flowers. No matter how high she flew she could see them, because she was an eagle and they have eyesight like, well, eagles. And of course, seeing flowers wasn't enough. She had to fly down and smell them, which meant she got a lot of stones thrown at her because humans do not feel comfortable about gigantic eagles landing in their gardens and trying to talk to them about their roses.

When she reached Transylvania Waters, she soared high above its ring of dangerous clouds,[32] took a deep breath and drifted down into the city. She landed on the lead roof of one of Castle Twilight's taller, more deserted towers and fell fast asleep.

[32] *See next chapter.*

The Floods drove north-east into the dark bit of Europe, where all the trees are black and people like cuckoo clocks so much they actually buy them. At each border crossing Mordonna clicked her fingers and the officials ushered them through into the next country.

Finally the campervan stopped at the foot of a great mountain range.

'You know what's on the other side, don't you?' said Winchflat.

'Really flat stuff with no mountains at all?' said Satanella.

'More mountains, probably,' said Nerlin. 'See, you should have let me do the driving.'

'Transylvania Waters,' said Mordonna. 'I can feel it calling me.'

'Oh, is that what it is?' said Nerlin. 'I thought it was all the wretched beetroot soup we've been eating.'

'If I remember my geography lessons,' said the Queen, 'there is no road as such into the country, just donkey tracks.'

'Mother, it was a very long time ago when you were at school,' said Mordonna. 'Things have changed.'

'Really?'

'Yes, your husband, my father, got rid of all the donkey tracks years ago.'

'You mean there's proper roads now?'

'Did I say that?' said Mordonna. 'No, he just got rid of the donkey tracks.'

'It's not a problem,' said Winchflat. 'I told you the campervan could go anywhere and so it can.'

He pressed two buttons and a big red knob

and they slowly lifted into the air. A small dog who was in the middle of lifting his leg on one of the van wheels fainted in surprise. So did the old lady holding the dog's lead.

The van rose silently above the trees and vanished into the clouds that always covered the mountain tops.

The clouds came halfway down the mountain, but only on the outside of Transylvania Waters. It had been like that for as long as anyone could remember. There were people over ninety years old who had never seen the mountain tops.

The clouds had been put there by the first wizards to settle in Transylvania Waters, to keep outsiders from coming into their country. For the clouds were not simple collections of fluffy water vapour like they are everywhere else. These clouds contained sleeping gas so that anyone climbing up into them fell asleep long before they reached the summit. It didn't take long for humans to learn to stay away. Sheep never learned, though, and the misty hillsides are dotted with sleeping sheep, some

of whom have been there for centuries.

'Wind up all the windows,' said Winchflat as they rose higher towards the mountain tops. 'I knew those fog lights would come in handy.'

'Look at all those sheep,' said Satanella to Brastof. 'I'd love to get out and chase them.'

'Getting out would not be good,' warned Winchflat. 'You would fall as fast asleep as they are.'

'Well, couldn't we open the window a bit and bark at them?' said Satanella.

'Yeah,' said Brastof. 'Brilliant. I aren't barfed at a sheep for two hundred years.'

'Don't you mean barked?' said Betty.

'That too,' said Brastof.

'Do not open the window or we will all fall asleep,' said Winchflat.

'Listen, darling,' said Mordonna to Satanella, 'when we get settled again, I'll get you a sheep of your own and you can bark at it all day.'

'Wow,' said Satanella.

'Can we barf at it too?' said Brastof.

‘If you hose it down afterwards,’ said Mordonna.

They came over the last rise and out of the clouds. It wasn’t gradual like normal clouds, but a sudden flat wall of fog. For a few seconds the front of the van was out in the cold clear air while the back was still hidden in mist. Then they were completely free and there it lay stretched out before them.

The deep sunless grey valley that was home.

Transylvania Waters.

Mordonna and Nerlin felt their blood surge with joy. Queen Scratchrot, although looking younger, had no blood left, but she felt her empty veins tingle.

Twenty-three years had passed since they had left the land of their birth. And every single day of those twenty-three years, Mordonna had closed her eyes for a few moments and brought back the memories of its wet grey valleys and waterfalls of acid rain.

She could see, far off in the distance, the brown fog of the evening rise out of Lake Tarnish and crawl towards the city, eating into everything as it passed, as it had done since the dawn of time.[33] The spires of the castle, green with verdigris, poked through the fog like the legs of a dead spider. It was the most beautiful sight the Floods had ever seen.

---

[33] *Actually it hadn't, because there hadn't been a city there at the dawn of time and the fog had only been acid brown since the Industrial Revolution. Before that, it had been a happy fog full of songbirds and butterflies.*

Even Mildred Flambard-Flood and the children, who had never seen their parents' homeland, stood in silence as they felt its magic calling out to them, inviting them down into the only true place on Earth where wizards and witches could be completely free.

'How could we have stayed away so long?' said Nerlin, putting his arm round Mordonna's shoulder.

'How could we have ever left such a paradise?' she replied, tears filling her eyes as she watched far below the little dots that she knew were the Evening Moths crashing into Lake Tarnish, overcome by its wonderful toxic fumes.

'Because of your stinky stupid father,' said the Queen.

'Yes,' said Mordonna. 'Since he took over, Transylvania Waters has ceased to be paradise.'

'True, and I blame myself for marrying him and bringing him here,' said the Queen. 'When my father was King, life was wonderful.'

'Then we must make it wonderful again,' said

Nerlin, so moved by seeing his homeland that he forgot all about sulking.

Transylvania Waters is surrounded on every side by tall mountains.[34] The slopes below the clouds on the outside, facing away from the country, are soft and green with grass and bushes and pretty birds sipping nectar from exquisite wild flowers and all that sort of fairy story rubbish, but those that face inwards are bare and rough and devoid of all life apart from the Night Vultures, a unique species that not only eat dead things, but will actually dig them up to do so.[35]

There is one other type of creature living on the Transylvania Waters side of the mountains. There is one on each mountain and they live in

---

[34] *Of course it's on all sides – otherwise it wouldn't be surrounded.*

[35] *This is why Transylvania Waters long ago gave up with cemeteries. You'd bury your dead granny and by the next day the Night Vultures had dug her up and eaten her. Most homes now have a huge dinner plate on the roof, which saves both the inhabitants and the vultures a lot of digging. The birds are known locally as the Funeral Directors.*

caves just below the summit. They are the Crones, old ladies with no living relatives who shun society and live their remaining years in deep meditation and complete isolation.[36]

When a Crone knows she is about to die, she lights a fire and down in the valley fights break out

[36] *Apart from the first Thursday of each month when they get together and play bingo.*

among the crowd of old ladies waiting to take the dead crone's place. The winner is then given a pair of warm socks, a sealed box containing a small bonfire and a box of matches to signal when she is dying, and sent off up the mountain. Quite often, because of their arthritis and the steep, rough terrain, they don't make it as far as the cave. After the Night Vultures have tidied them away, there is another old lady fight to choose her replacement. This can take weeks. In 1937 it took fifteen fights before an old lady actually made it up to the empty cave.

Winchflat brought the campervan down in front of one of the Crone Caves. By a wonderful coincidence, the sort of coincidence you usually only get in books, the Crone living there had once worked for Queen Scratchrot.

'I smell the Queen,' she said.

'Is that you, Quenelle,' said the Queen from the back of the van, 'my faithful old Armpit Cleaner?'

'It is, your majesty,' said the old lady, her eyes filling with tears. 'Oh, how I missed you when you

left. The King took a new wife and she was so cruel to all your faithful servants.'

'A new wife?' said the Queen. 'Who?'

'She was not from our country,' said Quenelle. 'She was from Bavaria.'

'Not the Countess Slab,' said the Queen, rattling with laughter. 'Don't say it was her.'

'Yes, your majesty,' said the old lady, 'and a bigger, wobblier, crueller, horribler, smellier person I never did meet.'

'But seriously rich, though,' said the Queen.

'Indeed, my lady.'

'I have heard, though, that she sings like a bird,' said the Queen. 'Is that true?'

'Oh yes, your majesty. She sings like a bird and does so from dawn till sunset,' said Quenelle. 'But the bird is a chicken.'

'I am sorry you and my other servants suffered so, but to be honest the two of them deserve each other.'

'Indeed, your majesty. They have made each other's lives complete misery,' said Quenelle. 'And

may I say, your majesty, you are looking younger than ever.'

Then Quenelle asked politely and the rest of the family turned away while the Queen lifted her arms and once again her old servant licked her armpits clean, as she had first done when Queen Scratchrot had been a baby.

'As sweet as ever,' said Quenelle, which made everyone else feel like throwing up.[37]

Crones live on a diet of snow and gruel, so Mordonna closed her eyes and did the Dinner Spell Number 437 – the banquet special. Over dinner they discussed their next moves.

'There are many who will welcome you back with open arms,' said Quenelle. 'I would imagine that, after years with Countess Slab, even the King would be happy to see you again. And if you think about it, there's probably only one person who won't be overjoyed to see you and that's the Countess herself.'

'Happy?' said the Queen. 'I'll teach him happy. If it wasn't for him we would never have had to leave all those years ago. Oh no, I want double, triple, quadruple revenge with extreme pain and humiliation. I want to see him tied naked to a cow with stinging nettles taped to his naughty bits and paraded through the streets of the town with barbed

---

[37] *Including me and everyone at my publisher.*

wire wrapped all round his bottom. I want him locked in the Transylvania Waters Big Brother House for six months with seventeen brain-dead teenagers who talk about nothing but the fluff in their tummy buttons. I want him covered in Vegemite and locked in a cage with fifty hungry poodles. I want so many horrible and nasty things done to him that I could write a big book about it.'[38]

'But don't they say "to err is human, to forgive divine"?' said Nerlin.

'First of all, I am not human. I am a witch,' said the Queen. 'And second, whoever said that was a complete idiot. They also, and this is probably a completely different "they", say "revenge is sweet".'

'But, but, what about "forgive thine enemies" and all that,' said Nerlin, who was quite a gentle soul underneath his gentle exterior.

---

[38] *A few years later the Queen did write the book* Dead Kings Don't Wear Crowns *and it was the bestselling title in the whole of Transylvania Waters' publishing history, outselling the other three books published there by ten to one.*

'Well, "revenge is a dish best served cold", as *they* say, and he's going to be very cold when I'm finished with him,' said the Queen. 'I was going to say the King won't know what hit him, but where's the fun in that? The King will most definitely know what hit him. ME!'

'Wow, Granny,' said Morbid. 'You are so cool.'

'Yes, I am, aren't I,' said the Queen. 'And if you are good, I'll let all you kids help me.'

'Brilliant.' Morbid and Silent gave each other a high-five.

'We will form the King Quatorze Humiliation Society,' said the Queen. 'And turn his stupid new wife into a bouncy castle.'

'Of course, there is another problem,' said Mordonna. 'And I certainly don't want any of my family risking their lives to deal with it.'

'What's that then?' said Nerlin.

'The Hearse Whisperer.'

'Oh, yes, I'd forgotten about her,' said Nerlin. 'Winchflat, anything on your sensors?'

'Well, she is either circling in the sky above us,' said Winchflat, 'or else there's a moth stuck on my antenna.'

'You're sure she's not still on Tristan da Cunha?'

'No, according my printout, she actually came back to Transylvania Waters a little while ago, and then went back to Tristan da Cunha and then left, but I'm not sure where she went next.'

'Let's just go with the moth idea, for the moment,' said Mordonna. 'We've enough to think about slipping back into the country. Besides, if Quenelle is right, we'll have plenty of people prepared to hide us while we work out what to do.'

'We could always go back and live in Acacia Avenue,' said Betty, who was missing her best friend Ffiona.

'I don't know about everyone else,' said Nerlin, 'but I've had enough of living amongst humans. They're just too weird and difficult.'

Everyone else felt the same, though they

did agree with Betty that their human friends the Hulberts had been OK.

'Mother, you are not going to kill the King, are you?' said Mordonna. 'It's not that I like him or would mind him being annihilated or anything like that, but I will not have my children involved in killing things.'

'Oh my goodness no,' said the Queen. 'He will end up living in a windowless stone hovel on a tiny remote Scottish island with three sheep, six clumps of grass and the Countess Slab, and they will both live miserably ever after for a very, very, long time with nothing to eat but seaweed and their own hair. No, it's all the stuff that is going to happen to him between now and then that the children can help me with.'

'And I'll tell you something,' she added. 'It will sure beat the hell out of Playstation.'

The sun doesn't so much as set over Transylvania Waters as get smothered by its brown smog. Then night falls with a soft thud. A few lamps twinkled in the darkness, going out one by one as

the population went to bed. The silence was really quiet, broken only by the occasional loud pop as a Lake Tarnish fish exploded, having swum too close to the surface.

'That is the most beautiful darkness I have ever seen,' said Mildred. 'The darkness inside my grave was lovely, but it was nothing compared to this.'

Since the verandah they had sat on at the end of every day in Acacia Avenue had been blasted into dust, the family were sitting together outside Quenelle's cave on a carpet of dried twigs and toadstools. It was the first time in weeks that everyone felt completely relaxed as Transylvania Waters worked its magic on their weary bodies.

Mordonna stirred her warm blood slurpie with a dried nightingale. 'Well,' she said, 'tomorrow we will go home.'

CHAPTER 17

'By the way,' said Mildred, as Mordonna blew out the last candle. 'I'm going to have a baby.'

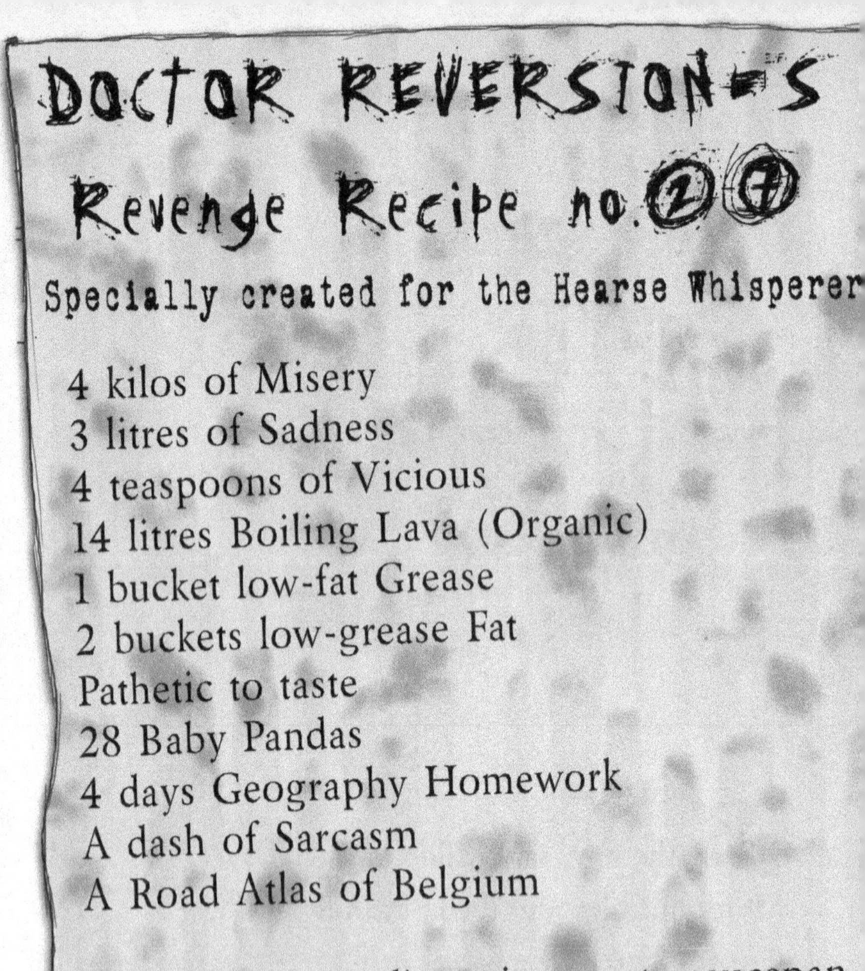

DOCTOR REVERSION'S

Revenge Recipe no. 27

Specially created for the Hearse Whisperer

4 kilos of Misery
3 litres of Sadness
4 teaspoons of Vicious
14 litres Boiling Lava (Organic)
1 bucket low-fat Grease
2 buckets low-grease Fat
Pathetic to taste
28 Baby Pandas
4 days Geography Homework
A dash of Sarcasm
A Road Atlas of Belgium

Put all the ingredients in a rusty saucepan and boil until the lid of the saucepan and the spoon have melted into the mixture. Do NOT allow to cool before injecting into the patient's ears with a VERY LARGE BLUNT RUSTY needle.
Run away very quickly.

DOCTOR REVERSION'S

Special Eco-Friendly Psychotherapy treatment boot

DOCTOR REVERSI

Special Eco-Friendly Psychotherapy treatment Slipper

NOWHERE
The Land that, like, time didn't forget, man, but just got bored with and wandered off.
gary krishna
BARRY krishna
harry krishna
the cool one's yurt
hairy krishnc
Like, a Tree

The Cool Pool

LIKE, A BIG COOL EMPTY SPACE WHERE, LIKE, NOTHING HAPPENS

everybody else's yurt

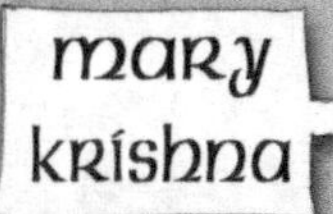

Have you read all of these brilliant books yet?

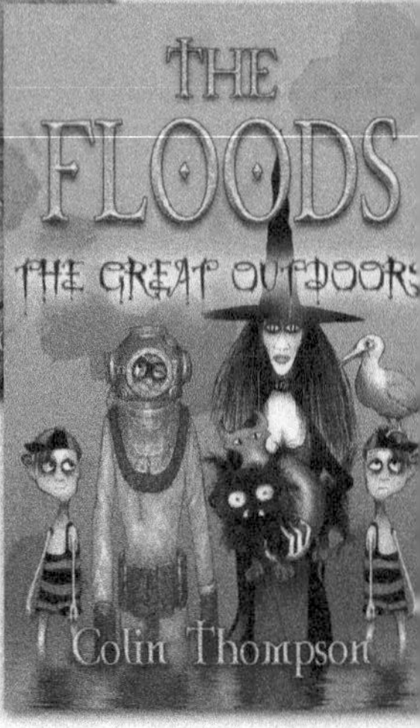

THE FLOODS
NEIGHBOURS
Colin Thompson

THE FLOODS
PLAYSCHOOL
Colin Thom

THE FLOODS
HOME & AWAY
Colin Thompson

THE FLOODS
SURVIVOR
Colin Thompson

THE FLOODS
PRIME SUSPECT
WANTED
THE FLOODS GANG
F.S.I
Colin Thompson

THE FLOODS
THE GREAT OUTDOORS
Colin Thompson

If the answer is NO, how lucky are you with all this incredible stuff to look forward to?

If the answer is YES, how clever are you?

AND, of course, don't forget to TOTALLY INCREASE your FLOODS ENJOYMENT by reading this HUGE, FULL COLOUR picture book

In ALL GOOD bookshops now and even in some BAD, WICKED and NASTY ones too.

Read on for a special preview of

THE FLOODS 8:

Better Homes and Gardens

'Are you dead?'

'What?'

'I said, are you dead?' said the vulture. 'Only we can't eat you if you're still alive.'

'That's good to know.'

'Yes, because we are carrion eaters and that means dead stuff,' said the vulture. 'Not dying or nearly dead, can't do that. We have to hang around until you're completely dead, preferably after a week or two when you're nice and ripe.'

'I am not dead,' said Valla.

'You sure?'

‘Of course.’

‘You look dead,’ said the vulture.

‘Well it’s nice of you to say so, but no, I am not dead.’

‘Not even a little bit?’

‘Not at all,’ said Valla, ‘and I’m not nearly dead either. Nor am I planning to be.’

‘What about her?’ said the vulture, pointing at Mildred Flambard-Flood. ‘She must be dead. I mean, look at her.’

‘Gorgeous, isn’t she?’ said Valla, ‘but happily still alive.’

‘And her?’ said the vulture, pointing at Queen Scratchrot.

‘Alive.’

‘So none of you are dead?’

‘No.’

‘Or planning to be in the near future?’

‘No.’

‘Do you not realise, you stupid bird,’ said Quenelle, running out of the cave and shaking her fist at the vulture, ‘who these people are?’

'Of course I do,' said the vulture. 'They're a bunch of half-dead hippies.'

'They are the Floods, the true Kings and Queens of Transylvania Waters,' said Quenelle. 'If they were dead, which they are not, you would not be worthy to even so much as nibble their toes, never mind eat them.'

The vulture buried her head in her wings and turned away.

'I feel so ashamed,' she said. 'Please forgive me, but I wasn't born when they left here so I had no way of knowing.'

Will the Floods take their rightful place as rulers of Transylvania Waters? Or will King Quatorze and the Hearse Whisperer finally get rid of them – once and for all?

Out now!

If you liked this book, there's heaps more stuff to check out at